TWO FRIENDS, ONE DOG, AND A VERY UNUSUAL WEEK

For Longfellow Elementary
—S.L.T.

To Riben, Amy, Jay, Don, and Alex
—V.V.

Published by
PEACHTREE PUBLISHING COMPANY INC.
1700 Chattahoochee Avenue
Atlanta, Georgia 30318-2112
PeachtreeBooks.com

Design and composition by Adela Pons
Edited by Catherine Frank

Printed in February 2023 at Maple Press, York, PA, USA.
10 9 8 7 6 5 4 3 2 1
First Edition
ISBN: 978-1-68263-516-2

Cataloging-in-Publication Data is available from the Library of Congress.

SARAH L. THOMSON
Illustrated by VIN VOGEL

TWO FRIENDS, ONE DOG, AND A VERY UNUSUAL WEEK

PEACHTREE
ATLANTA

CHAPTER 1

Emily Robbins's apartment building had three floors.

Except you could also say it had four.

The first floor was where Mr. Armand lived. He was the building manager. He fixed the radiators when they broke, told everyone where to leave their recycling, and talked to the chickens that he kept in the backyard.

On the next floor were the Pinkneys. Mrs. Pinkney liked to leave notes. Notes in the stairwell. Notes on the mailboxes. Notes on the fence by the recycling bins.

PLEASE REPLACE LIDS ON BINS.
PLEASE REMEMBER THAT YOUR FLOOR IS SOMEONE ELSE'S CEILING.
CHICKENS SHOULD NOT ROOST ON RADIATORS. PLEASE.

Emily always wondered when Mrs. Pinkney put these notes up, because she hardly ever saw her around the building—or her two kids, Jonah and Penelope, even though Penelope was in Emily's class at school.

The only time Emily had gotten a glimpse inside their apartment had been the year she was a Brownie and had knocked on their door to ask if they wanted to buy any Girl Scout cookies.

Mrs. Pinkney was very tall and very thin and very pale. Even her hair was very light blond and lay meekly and smoothly against her head. When she had opened the door, her white dress matched her skin and didn't have one speck of dust or dirt.

"Oh no," she said when she heard about the cookies. "We don't eat sugar here."

She closed the door quickly.

Emily's father said that was obviously the reason for all the notes. "Chronic sugar deprivation," he explained. "It's made her oversensitive to noise. And other people. And life."

Emily's mom told him to hush.

On the third floor were Emily, her mother, and her father. Emily's mother had black hair that was almost always in a ponytail. She cooked macaroni and cheese from a box. Her father had brown hair that was always too long because he hated going to get it cut, and he cooked lasagna and curried chicken and potstickers.

Emily's mother worked on computers in a big building downtown. Her father taught seventh grade. He had promised her that when she got to middle school, she could pretend not to know him.

The top floor of their building, the one above Emily and her family, was empty.

That's why you could say there were four floors. But the fourth one wasn't an empty apartment. There was nothing to make the space into somewhere to live—no kitchen or bedrooms, no sinks or bathtubs. Nothing but a big stretch of dusty wooden floor and a roof overhead that was really the roof of the whole building.

Sometimes Mr. Armand went up to make sure that no windows were broken and that there weren't any holes in the roof. If Emily asked, he'd let her come along.

She liked it up there. While Mr. Armand checked the windows and peered at the roof with a flashlight, Emily would spin in slow circles. She would trace crescents in the dust with the toe of her shoe and imagine the things someone could do up here.

Rollerblade races. Lego creations that could go in the *Guinness Book of World Records*. Scribbly murals all over the walls. Riding bikes in a giant circle, leaving ghostly tracks in the dust.

Dancing to music. Telling secrets. Laughing so hard and so loud that all your muscles felt weak and your joints got wobbly and you'd have to fall over. Nobody would tell you to quiet down or hang up your coat or do your homework or set the table.

You could do all of those things in a place like this, Emily thought.

If you just had somebody to do them with.

CHAPTER 2

It was a Saturday, and Emily was curled up on the window seat in the living room, waiting for her mother to take her to soccer practice. Through the window, she watched a black van pull up to the curb. Two muscly men in dark T-shirts opened its back doors.

Emily had seen what goes into and out of moving vans before. Mattresses and chairs and tables and lamps and lots and lots of cardboard boxes. Nothing very exciting.

Except this particular van didn't seem to be holding much of that. All Emily could see inside it was a chair.

An armchair covered in moss-green velvet with a high back and sides that sort of curved around so that anyone who sat there would be in their own little green velvet cave.

MOVING

Like the person who was sitting in it right now.

The only part of that person Emily could see clearly was a single skinny leg with a foot encased in a high-top sneaker.

The sneaker was covered in silver sequins and tied by a purple ribbon.

The two moving men took hold of the chair and lowered it gently to the sidewalk. They acted as if this were just part of the job to them, as if they unloaded armchairs with people in them every day.

Emily leaned out of the open window, trying to see better.

"Time to go!" her mother said, coming into the living room from the kitchen. "Hop up, shake a tail feather, let's get going, let's not be late, come on, Emily, get a move on!"

That was what Emily's mother always said, even when (like now) Emily had been the one waiting for her.

She followed her mother down two flights of stairs and out onto the sidewalk. There she discovered that the person in the armchair was a girl. She was still there. In the chair. On the sidewalk.

A big red backpack with buckles instead of zippers sat next to the chair. It was so full it was bulging.

Emily slowed down to get a look at the girl.

At first it was hard to tell if the armchair was huge or the girl was tiny. She sat so far back, deep in the chair, that Emily could only get a glimpse of her. She saw black hair that frizzed around the girl's head and eyes that were turquoise blue.

When those eyes met Emily's, they lit up as if there were an electric spark inside them. But the rest of the girl did not move.

Not an inch.

Emily did not think that her mom had spotted the girl at all. She was walking to the car and digging her keys out of her purse and telling Emily to catch up and saying hi to Mr. Armand, who had just hurried out of his first-floor apartment.

Mr. Armand waved to Emily's mom, but Emily could tell that he wasn't really paying much attention.

He was rushing toward the girl, calling, "You are here, you are here!"

"Of course I'm here," the girl answered. "I couldn't be anywhere else and still give you a hug, could I?"

The answer could have sounded really snotty, Emily thought, but it didn't. The girl bounded out of the chair and hugged Mr. Armand around his soft, squishy middle. She had a gap between her two front teeth that you could have slipped a penny into.

"Emily, hop in the car, it's very disrespectful to the coach and the other players to be late, goodbye, Mr. Armand, see you soon!" Emily's mother said.

As Emily climbed into the car, she heard the girl say, "And Otto's here too!" Then came a really loud whistle.

A giant black dog bounded out of the back of the van. He jumped up to put his front paws on Mr. Armand's shoulders and gave his face a slobbery lick.

Emily had decided by then that the chair was huge and the girl was tiny. The dog made her look tinier still.

Mr. Armand danced a waltz with the dog while the moving men shut the doors of the van and the girl talked and waved her hands like the conductor of an orchestra and Emily's mom drove the car away.

CHAPTER 3

That evening, Emily sat at the kitchen counter with her mother, trying the latest batch of her father's cinnamon-chip cookies. (Coconut for crispy edges and moist insides.)

As they ate, Emily listened to the noises overhead.

Footsteps. A door opening and closing. Something dragging across the floor.

"Hmm. The coconut makes them a little chewy," Emily's mother was saying. "Is someone moving in upstairs? When did they fix up that top floor?"

"I kind of like them chewy," Emily said. "But I liked the kind with ground-up almonds too."

"Maybe almonds *and* coconut?" her father said thoughtfully. "I saw some workmen heading upstairs last week."

The noises had to have something to do with the girl she had seen in the green chair, Emily thought. The girl with the dog.

"Can I take some cookies to the new people?" she asked her parents. "To say hello?"

A few minutes later, with a paper plate of cookies in her hand, Emily stood on the fourth-floor landing, staring at the door that led into the attic.

She lifted a hand to knock. Then she hesitated.

It was silly to be nervous. She just wanted to see if they had a new neighbor. To say hi. To be friendly.

"To make friends, you have to be friendly," her mother was always saying.

Emily's hand had fallen back down by her side. She lifted it up again and tapped lightly on the door.

It flew open at once.

"Hi!" said the girl standing in the doorway. "Salutations! Like Charlotte says. You know Charlotte, right? *Charlotte's Web*? Charlotte is an *Araneus cavaticus*—that's a barn spider. Did you know that the biggest spider of all is the Goliath birdeater? They don't actually eat birds that often.

They do eat mice, though. It's a good thing there wasn't one of those in the barn with Wilbur, or Templeton would have been toast! Their legs can stretch over a foot long. Wouldn't it be amazing to see one tap dance?"

Emily held the plate of cookies out in front of her, as if it were a dam that could block the flood of words.

"Thanks!" the girl said cheerfully. She took the plate. "Cookies! Cookies are a very good form of salutation. Do you want to come in? I figured you did, because you knocked on the door. But maybe you just came to deliver cookies. Or maybe you like knocking. Do you?"

Emily nodded. She had delivered cookies. Then she shook her head. She did not like knocking. Well, not particularly. She didn't hate it. But she didn't go around doing it for fun.

"You can come in *and* have some cookies," the girl decided. "And you can knock on the other side of the door if you'd like. That's Otto. He won't have any cookies. They don't agree with him."

She balanced on one leg and pointed a toe at the big black dog who was standing a bit behind her. Then she backed into the room. Emily got a good look at the dog and stayed in the doorway.

"Oh," she said. "Does he jump?"

Emily liked to pet dogs on the street and visit with them at other peoples' houses. But she'd never had one of her own. Her mom was allergic.

And she'd never met a dog as big as Otto. He sat and regarded Emily out of eyes that were only a little glossier than his black coat.

"Certainly he jumps!" declared the girl. "Once when we were in Peru, he jumped over a fence six feet high and into a rushing river to rescue a baby llama. But he doesn't jump up on people, if that's what you're asking."

And indeed, the dog didn't. He didn't actually have to jump to lick Emily's face—he just stretched his neck a little and slurped with a large pink tongue.

Emily wiped her cheek and glanced around the attic.

It had not changed much since the last time she'd been up there with Mr. Armand. The only thing that had been removed was the dust. Now the floor was shiny and the window glass was so clean it hardly seemed to be there.

At the far end of the room was the green chair. Next to it sat the girl's bulging red backpack and a heap of something that looked like green-and-yellow yarn.

Nearby, under a window, were two silver dog bowls, one filled with food and one with water.

And that was all.

"We heard the noises and thought maybe somebody was moving in," Emily said.

"Somebody is!" the girl said enthusiastically.

She stood with the plate of cookies in her hand, feet in their silver sneakers planted on the smooth, shiny floor. Only one of the shoes was laced with a purple ribbon. The other was tied with a piece of grubby string.

One sock was knee-high and striped red and green. The other was black and in a heap around the girl's ankle. She had on cut-off shorts and a purple T-shirt.

The girl's black hair zigzagged around her face in corkscrew curls. It almost seemed as if those curls could crackle with electricity. Her skin was golden brown, like tea with honey. Emily glanced briefly at her own hand, as pale as milk. Even in the summer, she never got tan. And her dark brown hair hung smooth and flat to her shoulders, nothing like the other girl's bouncy ringlets.

But the main thing Emily noticed about this new girl was that she wore a smile so big it shut her eyes into bright turquoise slits.

"I'm Rani," the girl said. It was a pretty name, one Emily had never heard before. First *Rah*, and then *Nee*. "It means *queen*. Can you help me with a hammer?"

CHAPTER 4

In a flash, Rani was on the other side of the room. She picked up a hammer from the seat of the green chair and put the cookies down in its place. Emily shortly found herself reaching into a side pocket of the backpack to hand Rani a nail at least two inches long.

Rani set the nail in the wall at eye level. Then she swung the hammer. *Bam!* "So you know my"—*bam!*—"name now." *Bam!* "What's yours?" *Bam!* The final blow from the hammer had bent the nail into a hook. Rani skipped to the next wall.

"Emily," Emily answered. She took a handful of nails from the backpack and followed Rani. "How come your dad's not doing this?"

"Don't have one," Rani answered sunnily. *Bam!*

"Oh." Emily felt herself blush. Had it been a dumb question? But Rani did not seem upset or embarrassed. So Emily tried again. "What about"—*bam!*—"your mom?" *Bam!* "She doesn't mind if you"—*bam!*—"hammer nails in the walls?"

"Certainly not. There!" The second nail was now a hook as well. Rani darted to the heap of yarn on the floor. She hung one end of it over the first nail and the other over the second. The yarn turned out to be a hammock that swung from the hooks in a bright swoop, stretching from wall to wall.

Rani rummaged in her backpack and pulled something out—a picture in the frame. Swiftly she banged another nail into the wall and hung the picture next to the hammock.

It showed a baby sitting in a hammock that looked very much like the one Rani had just strung up. The hammock in the picture dangled from two scrubby trees on the bank of a muddy river. The baby had a mop of black hair and was squinting and smiling in the bright sun.

"Perfect!" Rani leaped into the hammock and stretched out. She crossed her legs at the ankles and wiggled her toes inside their silver shoes. "Pass me those cookies, will you?"

Emily turned toward the chair in time to see the dog removing a single cookie from the plate, using only his front teeth.

"I'm afraid your dog just took one," she told Rani.

"Oh, he *will* do that." Rani shook her head at the dog. He walked a few paces away, sat down with his back to the two girls, and ate the cookie in one gulp.

"He knows perfectly well it will give him indigestion, but does he care? He does not."

Emily rescued the rest of the cookies and gave them to Rani. She settled the plate on her stomach and leaned back in the hammock, propping the heel of one foot on the toes of the other.

"There is nothing like a hammock for sleeping," Rani announced. "Have you ever tried it? The dreams are much better than the ones you get in an ordinary bed. Of course, I had the best dreams of my life when I was sleeping on an iceberg in Antarctica."

"You did?" Emily asked. Surely this girl was joking. Nobody ever slept on an iceberg. Did they?

"Of course I did. Shared it with three penguins and a polar bear. The polar bear wanted to eat the penguins, so Otto had to stay up all night to keep watch. But I went to sleep and had the loveliest dreams. All white and silver. Like dreaming inside the moon."

Emily's eyes went to the dog, who was licking cookie crumbs from his whiskers.

"You're joking," she said, relieved. She never liked that sticky, halfway feeling of wondering if you should laugh or not.

"Of course I am," Rani agreed. "There aren't any polar bears in Antarctica. Cookie?"

Emily sat on the floor beside the hammock, munching on a cookie. "Are you really going to stay up here?" she asked. It didn't seem like a place people could actually live, hammock or no hammock. Where was the kitchen? What about the *bathroom*? Emily would never dare to ask, but really—you had to have one.

"Curfinly," Rani said with her mouth full. She swallowed. "There are leopard seals, though."

"In the attic?"

"No, silly. In Antarctica. Pretty much as fierce as polar bears. You do *not* want to go swimming with them, let me tell you!"

Emily was quite sure she would never want to go swimming in Antarctica, leopard seals or no leopard seals. "Is the rest of your furniture coming soon?" she asked, still trying to understand how Rani's family was going to make this attic into a place fit for living.

"Oh, I suppose so." Rani sounded a bit annoyed by the idea. "I don't encourage it, but it does tend to follow me wherever I go."

"What does?" Were they still talking about leopard seals?

"Furniture. It's very persistent. These are excellent cookies." Rani handed Emily another one.

"But—" Emily's brain was starting to feel as if it had been twisted into a figure eight. "What about your mom? Where's she going to sleep?"

Rani's blue eyes widened as she stared at Emily in what looked like bewilderment. "Well, in Patagonia, of course. That's where she is."

CHAPTER 5

That night, Emily lay awake in bed, thinking of Rani swinging gently in her hammock, Otto snoring on the floor beneath her.

It couldn't be true about Rani's mother. Could it?

Rani made stuff up—that was for sure. She'd admitted it. She'd said herself that the thing about sleeping on an iceberg with three penguins and a polar bear wasn't true.

Which part exactly wasn't true, though? The penguins? The polar bear? Or the whole iceberg?

So probably the thing about Rani's mother being in Patagonia wasn't true either. They weren't quite lies, the things Rani said, Emily decided sleepily. They were . . . like poetry, sort of. Something that was supposed to sound pretty but not be an actual fact, not in the way it was a fact that 2 + 2 = 4, or that birds hatch out of eggs.

Emily fell asleep imagining her bed rocking gently back and forth.

On Sunday Emily did not get another glimpse of Rani. And she didn't hear any sound at all from the floor above. But that didn't stop her from thinking about her new neighbor.

The next morning she sat up with an idea tingling in her brain.

What if she asked Rani to walk to school with her?

Emily shoveled down her breakfast and got ready as quickly as she could. She had to wrestle her feet into her shoes. They were getting too tight and there wasn't very much room for her toes anymore, but she got them on at last, said goodbye to her mother, ran up to the attic, and knocked.

"Come in!" called a cheerful voice.

Emily tugged at the doorknob. "It's locked!"

"Otto, go open the door," she heard Rani say. "What kind of a butler are you?"

In a moment there was a click and the doorknob turned in Emily's hand. She pushed. The door opened. Otto was sitting just inside. He wagged his tail briefly.

"Um, thanks," Emily said. She patted him a little cautiously on the head. "Rani?"

Rani was sitting cross-legged in the green armchair, an empty paper plate on her lap. Her T-shirt today was a fiery red. The sleeves were black with silver polka dots and looked like they had come from a different shirt entirely.

"Your dad's cookies make a stupendifferous breakfast," she exclaimed cheerfully, wiping her mouth. "I'm sorry I don't have any for you. Otto ate yours. I told him not to, but he did."

Very delicately, Otto burped. He turned his head away.

"Oh," said Emily. "That's okay. I had oatmeal." She peered around the apartment.

There was no more furniture than there had been on Saturday. No bed other than the hammock. No sign of another person at all.

"Um," said Emily.

All of a sudden there was a nervous flutter high up in her stomach.

Emily knew what kind of a kid she was. The responsible kind. The kind teachers asked to take a message to the office. The kind who hung up her coat without being asked. The kind who had never been late to school. Not even once.

Rani was clearly a different kind of kid.

Maybe she would not want to walk to school with someone like Emily. But Emily was here, in the attic, standing right in front of Rani. She had to say *something*.

Something better than *um*.

"I was wondering," she said.

Rani nodded encouragingly, as if she were excited to hear what Emily had been wondering about.

"If you wanted. To walk to school?" Emily mumbled. "If you're going to my school, I could show you the way."

Although it seemed a little funny to think that a girl like Rani would need to be shown anything.

"School?" Rani asked. She tipped her head a little to one side. "What's school like?"

"Don't you know?"

"Course not. Never been." Rani licked her fingers one by one.

"But you *have* to go to school," Emily said. "There's a law."

"But there aren't any schools in Antarctica. Or in the rainforests of Borneo. Unless you think the orangutans want to learn long division. Maybe they'd like that." Rani paused, as if she were considering how much the orangutans would like math worksheets. "Orangutans can be very snobby, you know. They'd have tea parties and only invite their own particular friends. There were a lot of hurt feelings. Is your school like that, or can anybody come?"

"Anybody can come. I mean, any kid. Kids *have* to," Emily said again. "And I know that's not true, about the orangutans."

"Of course it's not true. Orangutans don't drink tea. What do all those kids do in school all day long?"

Suddenly Emily was not quite sure what anybody did in school all day long. "Learn stuff. I guess."

"Well, I already know stuff." Rani set the plate aside and jumped up. "But I don't mind learning more. I'll come and check it out." Rani snatched up her big red backpack. "Come on, Otto. Let's go to school!"

Everything that Rani did, she did at top speed. Emily found herself trailing both Rani and Otto down the stairs. "I don't think dogs can come," she said to Rani's back.

"I thought you said anybody could come!" Rani called back. "Anyway, orangutans mostly drink coffee."

Emily had been walking the four blocks between her apartment and the Henrietta Minnow School for five years, ever since she'd been in kindergarten and had held her mom's hand the entire way. Some days she walked by herself. Sometimes she met up with a friend from her class—Maureen Kenilworth, maybe, or Annie Park or Lena Horowitz.

But she'd never walked to school with somebody like Rani.

They passed the deli next door to the apartment building, and Rani waved to Mr. Rose, who was inside mopping the floor. He waved back and smiled as Rani snagged a shiny apple off the table out front and bit into it. She tossed a second one to Emily.

Emily caught it awkwardly. "Um . . . I don't have any money," she said.

"You don't need any! Right, Mr. Rose?" Rani grinned and skipped ahead, munching her apple.

A little alarmed, Emily glanced at Mr. Rose, but he didn't seem angry. "Sure thing, Rani!" he called after her.

While Emily was wondering if she was going to pay for the apples later, Rani darted into a bakery. She came out with a couple of cinnamon rolls and handed one to Emily. Then she shared her own with Otto.

No one at the bakery seemed upset, any more than Mr. Rose had been. And the cinnamon roll smelled amazing. Emily dropped her apple core into a trash can and took a bite, tasting sweetness all the way down to her toes.

Emily chewed while Rani skipped ahead and sang silly songs to babies in strollers, spun around streetlights, and ran up the front steps of apartment buildings so that she could slide down the railings.

"Keeping them polished!" she called cheerfully, patting her rear end.

They turned a corner and crossed a street and were now only half a block from the Henrietta Minnow School. Rani clapped her hands at the sight of the stone wall that ran around the school and enclosed the playground.

"Oh, perfect!" she cried out in delight. "You didn't say there was a wall!"

CHAPTER 6

In a moment, Rani was up on the top of the wall, striding confidently and waving at passersby.

Emily's mouth was full of cinnamon roll. She had to swallow before she could warn Rani. "Kids aren't allowed up there!" she called, hurrying along the sidewalk next to Otto. Rani's silver sneakers were several inches above the top of Emily's head.

"Not allowed?" Rani turned a neat cartwheel, her shoes flashing. "Who says?" she asked while upside down.

"The teachers!" Emily gasped in dismay. "Oh, Rani, you'll get in trouble. Please! They really don't like kids being up there."

Rani had landed her cartwheel. She stood squarely on both feet, hands on hips, and peered down at Emily. "Well, that's not fair. Why do the teachers get the wall all to themselves? I bet they're not even good at cartwheels." She looked toward the pair of wide iron gates that led into the playground. Next to the gates, the school flag snapped in the wind at the top of its pole.

"Race you!" Rani shouted and charged ahead.

Down on the sidewalk, Emily threw away the rest of her cinnamon roll and started off after her. How could such a tiny person be so fast?

She had to dodge around Penelope Pinkney and her mother. "Goodness, Emily, slow down! Manners!" Mrs. Pinkney said. "And what is that—dog! Dog! Why is there a dog here? Why isn't it on a leash? Shoo! Shoo!"

Penelope let out a little shriek as Otto brushed past.

Both gates had been propped open to let students and parents in. Just before she reached them, Rani stopped running. She plopped down to sit on the wall next to the flagpole, facing the playground and swinging her legs.

Emily hurried through the gates. "Rani? Please, you have to come down," she panted.

"Naturally," Rani agreed. "Everything that goes up must come down, and the gravity here is in perfect working order."

She twisted around to dig in her backpack and tug something out—a shiny black tube. She put it to her eye. Emily realized that it was a telescope.

"What an excellent view!" Rani exclaimed. "What's the tall building over there?"

"The Mayflower Hotel? Rani, really . . ."

"Is it shut up?"

"Yes, my dad said so. He says it's a shame. He says it's a cool old place. Please come down, Rani?"

"I will soon." Rani snapped the telescope shut. "I think I may have to put off going to school for a few days, though. Tell your teachers to enjoy walking on the wall."

Emily glanced around. Maybe nobody had noticed what Rani was doing.

But that was too much to hope for. Near the entrance to the school, Mrs. Pinkney stood talking to Mr. Cleary, the principal. The next moment he was hurrying across the playground toward Rani and Emily.

Emily winced. She hated to watch people get in trouble. It always made a squishy sensation grow in her stomach, right under her rib cage.

And it was going to be especially bad watching Rani get in trouble. Rani acted as if she didn't know what trouble was.

"Oh my. My goodness. What's happening here, Emily?" Mr. Cleary asked. He stared at Rani, still seated on the wall. "I don't think I know you. Do I?"

"My friend Emily brought me," Rani said as cheerfully as ever. "She said anyone could come, because it's not like a club where some people aren't allowed."

Mr. Cleary actually hesitated. Emily knew why. "Never exclude anyone," was a big rule at the Henrietta Minnow School. If someone wanted to play, you had to let them—even if the someone was Penelope Pinkney.

Then Emily's mind backtracked to what Rani had just said.

My friend Emily . . .

They were friends already? Rani and Emily?

She took a quick breath and spoke up. "I didn't get a chance to tell Rani about nobody being allowed to climb the wall," she said. "Sorry."

Emily braced herself as the uncomfortable feeling in her stomach swelled up toward her throat. Now she'd be in trouble too.

"Oh, Emily did say about the wall, but I really think the teachers should share with the children," Rani said earnestly. "It's not fair if they're the only ones who get to climb it."

Mr. Cleary shook his head. His wispy brown hair quivered anxiously.

"I think—I don't quite—teachers don't climb the wall," he said. "And furthermore—"

"Oh, they should!" Rani's eyes were wide with surprise. "You get such an excellent view from up here!"

She jumped down, landed lightly, and glanced at the gates. "Coming, Otto!" she called.

Mr. Cleary looked the same way. He twitched all over. Otto was sitting next to the flagpole. A kindergartener had draped herself over his back like a cape. Another was having his face licked.

"A dog! A dog on the playground!" Mr. Cleary gulped. "It's very dangerous to bring a dog onto a school playground!"

"It is?" Rani turned her head from side to side as if checking for threats. "What could hurt him? He's very brave. Once he drove a pack of coyotes away from our campsite in the Sonoran Desert. Still, I'm supposed to look after him. We'd better go. Thanks for walking me to school, Emily!"

With a cheerful wave, Rani set off. Otto offered each kindergartener one last lick and followed her out of the gates.

Mr. Cleary's expression was both alarmed and confused. "Emily, who was that girl?"

Emily stared after Rani.

"My new friend?" she answered. She hadn't meant to put a question mark at the end of that sentence. But somehow it was there.

CHAPTER 7

Emily did not see Rani again for a couple of days.

But she heard her.

Saws growling. Hammers bashing. Drills whirring.

Something was going on in the attic, that was for sure. Emily ventured upstairs to knock on the door a few times, but either Rani did not hear over all the racket, or she didn't feel like answering.

On Wednesday morning, Emily was looking out of her own apartment window when a pickup truck pulled up with a heap of glittering crystal in the back. Workers in hard hats hoisted it into the air, and the heap turned out to be an enormous chandelier. Emily watched, fascinated, as it disappeared through an attic window.

Someone else was watching too. Mrs. Pinkney stood in the tiny front garden of the apartment building and gazed at the chandelier going up, up, up, and inside.

The next day, Emily's father picked her up after school. When they got home, Mrs. Pinkney was sitting on the bench by the front door. Her son, Jonah, crouched nearby, peering into a bed of pansies.

Mrs. Pinkney stood up when Emily and her father arrived.

"Excuse me," Mrs. Pinkney said. "Do you know that . . ." She paused. "That new girl?"

"Up in the attic?" Emily's father said. "I haven't met her yet, but Emily has. Hey there, Jonah."

Jonah glanced up from the pansies but didn't answer. Emily had yet to hear Jonah Pinkney say a word. He was the quietest four-year-old she'd ever met. Solemnly he returned his gaze to the flowers. Emily caught a glimpse of one of Mr. Armand's chickens among the blossoms. She thought it was Carlotta.

Jonah took a small, green plastic figure out of one pocket and showed it to Carlotta, who pecked at it to see if she could eat it. Mrs. Pinkney turned her attention to Emily. Her entire face looked pinched.

"Is her family going to stay long?" she asked. "What do her parents do?"

"I don't know," said Emily.

Jonah reached a hand into the flowers to stroke Carlotta's feathery back. Mrs. Pinkney's face pinched tighter. "Is she in the same grade as you and Penelope?"

"I don't know," said Emily again.

"Hmmm," said Mrs. Pinkney. "Jonah, leave that filthy bird alone!" She took Jonah's hand, pulled him to his feet, and led him inside.

"Nice chatting with you too. Have a lovely day!" Emily's dad muttered under his breath as he and Emily followed.

Upstairs, Emily settled down in the window seat with her book (*Hatchet*, chapters twelve and thirteen to be finished by Friday). She opened it and stared at the words on the page, but she didn't read.

Instead, she wondered.

What would Mrs. Pinkney do if she found out that Rani was living in the attic all by herself?

For that matter, what would Emily's parents do?

Emily glanced out of the window. She yelped.

Rani waved. She was right on the other side of the glass, hanging upside down. Her bright orange T-shirt and tie-dyed pajama pants made her seem like a colorful spider, and her hair fluffed out around her face.

"What was that, hon?" Emily's father called from the kitchen.

"Nothing!" Emily flung the window open.

"Hello there," Rani said cheerfully as she swayed two stories above the ground. Now Emily noticed the harness that fit snugly around Rani's torso and the line that held her suspended from the attic window.

"What are you *doing*?" Emily asked.

"Inviting you to tea," Rani answered. "Unless you're like the orangutans and only drink coffee."

"But you're upside down!"

"Oh, I'll turn right side up for tea," Rani assured her. "But you'll have to take the stairs, I'm afraid. I only have one climbing harness."

She flipped herself over, braced her feet against the

brick wall, and began to walk up the side of the building as easily as if she were strolling on the ground.

Emily leaned out of the window to watch Rani until she was safely back inside. Then she jumped up, grabbed her shoes, wrestled her feet into them, asked her father if she could visit Rani, got a yes, and ran to the attic.

This time, Rani's door opened before Emily knocked. Otto was sitting inside.

Emily looked around and saw what all the noise had been about.

Along one wall of the attic there was now a loft halfway between the floor and the ceiling. A ladder rose up to it and a gleaming metal slide curved down from one end.

The chandelier that Emily had seen delivered hung from the ceiling. Light fell through its crystals and scattered tiny shards of rainbows across the floor.

Rani's head appeared over the edge of the loft. "Come up!" she called.

Emily climbed the ladder. The floor of the loft was scattered with cushions—some silk or satin, some covered in white fur, some embroidered with tiny mirrors. Red velvet curtains hung around three sides, making the space feel safe and secret.

Rani sat on a fuzzy green cushion. On a tiny table next to her, only a foot or so above the floor, was a teapot, two cups, and a plate of ginger cookies.

"I'm glad you're here," said Rani. "Otto doesn't drink tea." She poured a fragrant brown stream into one of the cups. "One lump or twenty-seven?"

"Rani! Did this stuff come out of that old hotel?"

Rani nodded. "Most of it. They weren't using it anymore."

"And did you build all this yourself?"

"Most of it," Rani said again. She took a sugar lump from her pocket and dropped it into Emily's cup. Then she dropped a second lump into her mouth, poured tea into her own cup, and gulped it down before the sugar could dissolve. "Let's try out the slide!"

CHAPTER 8

The slide swung Emily into a dizzying curve and dumped her onto a thick mattress at the bottom. Breathless, she scrambled back up the ladder to try it again.

Next Rani and Emily slid down together. Then Rani showed Emily a wide canvas sling that hung over one side of the loft. She called Otto, who stepped into the sling and let Rani buckle it around his chest and across his back. Rani turned a handle that pulled ropes through a pulley and hoisted Otto up into the air.

Otto didn't seem to mind as he rose, all four legs dangling. Once he reached the level of the loft, he stepped onto a platform. Rani, who had hurried up the ladder, unbuckled his harness.

The dog sniffed carefully all around, chose a huge pink cushion to curl up on, and gazed at Rani as if expecting something.

She gave him a ginger cookie. "But only one!" she warned him sternly.

Otto ate his cookie and watched Rani and Emily slide again and again and again.

"I wish we could do this all day," Emily said a little breathlessly after she'd climbed up to the loft for the fifth time. She flopped back on a soft red silk pillow.

"Why can't we?" Rani asked with her mouth full of cookie.

"Well, I have to do my homework. Reading."

"Huh. Reading," Rani said with a spray of crumbs.

"Don't you like reading?"

"Never saw much point. I'd rather be doing," Rani said. "But go on. Get your book. You can read up here."

Emily did. "What's it about?" Rani asked, eyeing the cover.

"A boy whose plane crashes in the wilderness. And he has to survive all by himself. With just a hatchet."

"Read to me."

Emily glanced at Rani in surprise. She had settled back down on her green cushion. She seemed serious.

"Okay." Emily opened the book and began to read about Brian hunting in the forest.

Reading went much quicker with a friend and a big dog listening and ginger cookies to eat whenever Emily was ready for a break. She got all the way to Brian's first successful fishing expedition before her voice began to creak.

"Not bad," Rani said. "Once my mom and I went fishing in Denali, and our jeep got chased by a herd of caribou."

Emily closed her book. "Where's Denali?"

"Alaska," Rani answered. "Did you know that caribou is another name for reindeer? So Santa's sleigh is actually pulled by flying caribou."

Emily was tempted to ask more about the caribou, but she didn't let herself get distracted. "Rani, were you really in Alaska?" she asked.

"Of course!" Rani flopped down on her back, stretched her feet up to the ceiling and wiggled her toes.

"With your mom?"

"Yep. You didn't think I was driving a jeep all by myself, did you?"

"And your mom's in Patagonia now?"

"Sure. She's a wildlife photographer. So she has to go where the wildlife is. Didn't I tell you that part?"

Emily shook her head.

"Well, she is. She travels all over the world to take pictures of animals. And she takes me with her. Has done ever since I was a baby. That's me in the picture."

Rani pointed one foot at the photo of the smiling baby that hung near her hammock. Emily glimpsed an electric kettle on the windowsill next to the chair. So that was how Rani had made the tea.

"She was tracking man-eating tigers in Bangladesh when she took that picture," Rani went on. "Of course they eat women too. And children. They aren't picky."

Emily stared. "And she took you with her?"

"Sure." Rani let her legs drop to the floor of the loft, one at a time. "I didn't get eaten."

"Well, I figured." Emily took another cookie. She felt as if everything was a little more solid now. Rani's mom didn't seem like such a will-o'-the-wisp, a ghost that flitted in and out of Rani's conversation. She was a real person with a real job, even if that job was a little, well, wild.

"So how come your mom didn't take you to Patagonia?" Emily asked.

"Oh, she did! But it's cold in Patagonia, and she's going to be camping out for a while, so I said I'd rather hop on an airplane and head up here to stay with Mr. Armand."

"And she just let you?" Emily was fascinated. It was only this year that her parents had allowed her to walk to school by herself. And Rani's mom let her fly home from Patagonia?

Also, she thought, it was too bad she hadn't known that Rani's mom was a wildlife photographer when Mrs. Pinkney had asked about Rani's parents. It might have helped.

Or maybe not.

"Listen, Rani," she said. "You know Mrs. Pinkney? Downstairs? She was asking a lot of questions about you."

Rani beamed. "That's nice. She must be friendly. Do you think she'd like to try the slide?"

Emily's imagination frizzled and failed at the idea of Mrs. Pinkney going down Rani's slide.

"No, I don't think so," she said. "And I don't think she's that friendly either. I think—"

A knock came on the door.

"Emily? Your dad says you're up here," Emily's mother called. "We've got to go shoe shopping before dinner. Come on, shake a tail feather!"

"Shoe shopping!" Rani could not have been more thrilled if Emily's mom had said they were going to a candy factory. A candy factory in Disneyland. "I can't wait!"

CHAPTER 9

Emily's mom was happy to meet Rani and said that she didn't mind if Rani joined them for shoe shopping. It was a little more complicated to explain to Rani that Otto could not come.

"He has *four* feet!" Rani pointed out. "He needs *twice* as many shoes!"

But at last she had been convinced that Otto would not enjoy himself, and the big dog had been left at home.

Rani did not consider it necessary to change out of her pajama pants. She just put on her silver shoes and scampered down the stairs with Emily behind her. They piled into the back seat of Emily's mom's car for the drive to the SuperSmartSaverMart.

Once they got there and were walking across the black parking lot, something buzzed loudly inside Emily's mother's purse. She sighed and dug her phone out of her bag.

"Oh, hello. No, I can't, it's my half day, I'm not at work, I'm—oh. You're kidding! Don't tell me that. *Please* don't tell me that. How? Please tell me how, no, don't tell me!"

Emily's mother turned away from the girls and covered one ear while holding her phone to the other. She groaned. "Well, then I have to, okay, all right, thirty minutes. All right!"

She ended her call and stuffed the phone back in her purse. "I'm so sorry," she said, turning back to the girls. "Work crisis. Some idiot mangled the mainframe and I've got to go in. Emily, I'm sorry."

"Why can't Emily and I shoe shop together?" Rani asked.

Emily's mom blinked. "Well, but . . ." She took out her phone again. "You're only nine years old. I don't think . . ."

"Oh, don't worry, Mrs. Robbins!" Rani said cheerfully. "One time I went to buy sandals in a street market in Rajasthan and someone was selling camels there too. They didn't need shoes. The camels. But I decided I'd rather have a camel than a pair of sandals. I named her Matilda. I thought we should probably go on a tour of a desert so she could visit with some friends. They were also camels. And I didn't get back for about a week. But it was fine. Absolutely fine. This store should be no problem at all."

Emily was not sure how Rani managed it, but she did. Somehow this story of Matilda the camel resulted in permission for Emily and Rani to go into the SuperSmartSaverMart and look at shoes until Emily's dad could come on the bus and take them home.

This was . . . exciting.

Emily thought it was, anyway.

She *did* need new shoes. She was tired of having scrunched toes.

And she'd never gotten to go into the SuperSmart-SaverMart by herself. Usually she was with her mom or her dad or both. And they were always hurrying her along or bustling her into line or warning "We're not buying that!" if Emily slowed down in the candy aisle.

Grown-ups never understood how nice it was just to gaze on rows and rows of silky-smooth chocolate bars in bright wrappers or buckets of gumballs, all rainbow colors. Just knowing there was all that candy in the world was a wonderfully satisfying feeling.

Now she and Rani would be able to go down the candy aisle as slowly as they pleased. They could stop to stroke fuzzy sweaters or hug squishable teddy bears. All on their own. With no one telling them to catch up or shake a tail feather.

It should be great. It *would* be great.

But Emily realized that it would be a little worrying too.

What would Rani do once they were inside the SuperSmartSaverMart? Emily had already figured out that Rani did not do things the way most people did.

In the attic, that was fun.

On the school playground, it had been kind of strange.

What would it be like in a store? Emily was still wondering about that as her mom took them to the entrance and hugged them and hurried back toward the car. She already had her phone up to her ear.

"Rani," Emily asked. "Have you ever been to a SuperSmartSaverMart before?"

"Nope!" said Rani. "I've been snorkeling on the Great Barrier Reef, though. Does that count?" The big glass doors whooshed open and she stood wide-eyed, gazing at the scene inside. "Oh. My. Do you think they have camels?"

"No," said Emily. "I'm pretty sure they have everything else, though."

CHAPTER 10

Shoppers hurried past, pushing bright orange carts loaded with clothes, groceries, toys, and pet food. One woman had a lamp and a potted plant in her cart. Another had three turquoise vases, a badminton racquet, and a giant box of toilet paper.

A clown in an orange polka-dot suit was standing just inside the doors. “Hello and welcome to the SuperSmartSaverMart,” he said and thrust a turquoise balloon in Emily’s face. He had a bright red smile painted across the lower half of his face. Underneath it, his real mouth was set in a flat line.

“Thank you for choosing the SuperSmartSaverMart. We want you to have whatever you want,” he told the girls.

When Emily was little, she'd been scared of the SuperSmartSaverMart clown. Now she took a balloon every time because she felt sorry for him. She always let her balloon go as soon as she was out of his sight. The high ceiling of the SuperSmartSaverMart was crowded with balloons that had lost half of their air, bobbing listlessly among the rafters as if they wanted to get out but didn't have the energy to try very hard.

"That's so nice of you!" Rani gave the clown a beaming smile. "I'm Rani. What's your name?"

She took a purple balloon and shook the clown's hand energetically.

"Uh . . . Rich." Rich the clown stared down in surprise at Rani's hand shaking his. "Most people don't ask."

"How funny!" Rani let his hand go. "We certainly will enjoy your store, even if you don't have any camels. It was very nice to meet you!"

She waved and strolled into the SuperSmartSaverMart. Emily followed.

It was perfectly fine to shake the hand of the SuperSmart-SaverMart clown, Emily thought. Of course it was. There wasn't anything actually wrong with it.

She'd just never seen anybody do it before.

"This is a very friendly store," Rani said as they walked past a giant display of umbrellas and a bunch of mannequins in ponchos.

"The shoes are this way." Emily pointed to the far corner of the store, where she could see a tower of shoeboxes stacked up halfway to the ceiling.

She glanced back to make sure Rich the clown wasn't watching and let her balloon go. Then she tugged Rani down an aisle lined with snack food and candy. She didn't feel like lingering, after all. It seemed important to get to the shoes as quickly as possible.

She almost told Rani to shake a tail feather.

A fussy toddler was sobbing in a cart as her mother scanned the snacks. Rani reached up to pluck a sparkly orange pinwheel from the top of a display of jelly beans. She handed it to the baby. "There, that will cheer you up!" she declared.

"Oh . . . thank you." The toddler's mother lowered her gaze to Rani in her orange T-shirt. "Do you . . . work here?"

"It's not work. It's fun!" Rani said, striding ahead. She snagged a package of caramels off a shelf. "I've never been to a store where they just want you to have anything you like. It's so nice of them!" She handed her purple balloon to Emily, tugged the bag open, and grabbed a handful of caramels.

"You can't eat those!" Emily yelped.

Rani stared at her in bewilderment.

"I can't?" She handed the open bag to Emily. "Oh, you're right. Caramels really aren't good for your teeth. I fed some to a beaver once and he got all his teeth stuck together. Do you know how hard it is to convince a beaver to brush his teeth?"

Rani jumped up to snag a big red bag of popcorn on a shelf just above her head. "This is better. Don't you think?"

In dismay, Emily clutched the bag of caramels in one hand and the string of Rani's balloon with the other. "No, Rani, I mean you can't eat *anything*!"

She was too late. Rani had already ripped the bag of popcorn open. She started walking again. "What do you mean? Rich said he wanted me to have everything I want. Right now I want some popcorn."

Emily scurried after her. "Yes, I know, but he meant he wanted you to *buy* everything you want. You still have to pay for stuff!"

Rani chomped and swallowed. "Oh, well, that's no problem. I have plenty of money."

"Really?" Emily's panic ebbed a little. If Rani could pay

for the popcorn and the caramels, they wouldn't get into too much trouble.

"Course I do. You didn't think my mom would go off to Patagonia and leave me with nothing, did you?" They'd left the snack aisle by now. Emily was relieved about that. They were walking by a display of cleaning supplies, and Rani was not likely to snatch a mop or a box of wet wipes off the shelf.

Emily hoped so, anyway.

"So there's nothing to worry about. Here, have some popcorn." Rani stuffed another handful into her mouth and tossed the bag to Emily.

CHAPTER 11

Emily wanted to explain that you had to pay for things *first* and eat them afterward, but she was distracted by the open bag of popcorn flying through the air. She dropped the caramels to try to snatch it. Popcorn sprayed up and fountained down around her like snowflakes in a movie.

Emily heard herself make a sound like *yeep!*

"Oops," Rani said. "Oh, but look—it's no problem." She darted up to a display of vacuum cleaners and tried to switch one on. "Rats, it's not plugged in. There!" She'd found an outlet and was crawling to it, holding the vacuum's power cord between her teeth.

Emily clutched the crumpled popcorn bag in one hand and Rani's balloon in the other. She revolved slowly and anxiously in place, scouting for outraged SuperSmartSaverMart employees in their orange smocks and name tags.

What did they *do* to you if you spilled popcorn all over their store? She'd never spilled anything in a store before. She didn't know what might happen.

They'd better get it all cleaned up before someone saw. But Emily couldn't clean up if her hands were full.

She thought about letting the balloon go, but it was Rani's, so maybe she shouldn't. Then Emily remembered what her dad used to do with balloons when she was little. She parked the popcorn on a nearby shelf and tied the balloon to one of her belt loops.

Meanwhile, the vacuum cleaner roared to life. Rani charged at the fluffy white morsels on the floor and Emily had to hop backward to save her toes.

While pieces of popcorn vanished inside the vacuum cleaner, Emily heard a faint voice. "Excuse me! Excuse me! Young ladies!"

Oh no.

Emily's heart began to beat faster. Rani's balloon bobbed above her head as she looked up to see a bald man wearing an orange smock, a brown mustache, and a heavy frown. His name tag read, "Hello, my name is . . ." But the written-in name had turned into a gray blur. She couldn't read it at all.

Emily bent down to start picking caramels up off the floor.

The SuperSmartSaverMart employee ignored her. "Young lady!" he said to Rani, raising his voice over the growl of the vacuum cleaner. "I can't allow you to use that!"

"It's no trouble!" Rani answered just as loudly.

To Emily's eyes, Hello-My-Name-Is-Blur seemed to get taller. His frown definitely got sterner and his mustache more menacing. "Young lady!" he bellowed.

The last piece of popcorn was sucked up. Rani switched off the vacuum cleaner. "No need to thank me," she told the employee. "I was glad to do it."

"Excuse me, is that vacuum cleaner for sale?" asked a new voice.

Emily turned to see the mom with the toddler in her cart. The baby waved her pinwheel at Rani.

"I was hunting for a vacuum cleaner, and that one looks very good!" the mother said. "It was so helpful to see a demonstration." She frowned a little at Rani in puzzlement. "Aren't you sort of young to work here, though?"

"Oh, they don't have to pay me. My pleasure!" Rani waved at the baby.

To her amazement, Emily found that she had a caramel in her mouth. She did not remember putting it there. It was large and extremely chewy.

Hello-My-Name-Is-Blur had transferred his attention to the toddler's mother. "Yes, of course it's for sale," he told her. His smile spread as smoothly as if his teeth had been buttered. "It's an expensive model, but more than worth the price. Here, I can put one in your cart for you. And who's this handsome young gentleman?" He put his face near the toddler, who frowned and whacked him on the nose with her pinwheel.

"That's my daughter, Elsie," the mom said.

Hello-My-Name-Is-Blur straightened up, rubbing his nose. "Yes. Well. Yes. Here you go. . . ." He seized a box holding a vacuum cleaner. "Young ladies, wait right there!"

Emily knew she'd have to explain to Hello-My-Name-Is-Blur that Rani hadn't meant to break the store rules. But she couldn't do it with a caramel in her mouth.

She chomped frantically as Hello-My-Name-Is-Blur heaved the vacuum cleaner into the cart. He narrowly missed whacking little Elsie in the head.

"Oh, that's okay. We don't need any help," Rani told Hello-My-Name-Is-Blur. She tugged on Emily's arm, pulling her toward the corner of the store where the stacked-up shoeboxes towered over the shelves. "You're welcome!" she called back.

And the employee let them walk away. Emily was amazed. He was so busy getting the vacuum cleaner safely in the cart and apologizing to Elsie's mom that he didn't even chase after them or demand their names or call their parents or anything.

She gulped and swallowed a mound of buttery sweetness so big it hurt a little going down. "Oh, Rani, you shouldn't have done that," she managed to say.

But to her surprise, she found that she was giggling as she remembered little Elsie and her pinwheel.

"Why not?" Rani asked, astonished. "If you make a mess, you should always clean it up. It's just good manners." They turned a corner and found themselves in an aisle full of bikes and tricycles and skateboards. "Of course, if you're having dinner with the king of England it's good manners to talk to the person on your right first and then on your left. So it all depends."

"Rani." Emily wiped her mouth on the back of her hand. "You haven't met the king of England. Have you?"

"No, but you never know. Hello, what are you doing there?"

CHAPTER 12

The person Rani had said hello to was a kid about four years old, standing by himself in the middle of the aisle, staring at a display of scooters. His eyes were wide with longing and there were no adults in sight.

"Are you a boy?" Rani asked him. "Or are you a *Homo floresiensis*? They only grew about three and a half feet tall, so you might be one of them. I always say it's best to ask."

"Rani, he's not a—whatever you said," Emily told her. "Jonah? Jonah Pinkney?"

The boy turned his wide brown eyes to her. His lower lip sagged. His chin began to quiver.

"Where's your mom?" Emily asked him.

Jonah's shoulders moved up about half an inch. Then they settled back down where they'd started.

"I think he's lost," she said to Rani. "We should tell somebody who works here. They'll help."

"We don't need to get help," Rani said. "We're *going* to help." Deftly she hefted a glittery purple scooter from the display and set it on the floor. "Hop on!" she told Jonah.

"Rani!" Emily nearly wailed. "I told you—they don't *actually* want you to have whatever you want. You're not supposed to take stuff!"

"I'm not taking it. I'm borrowing it!" Rani boosted Jonah onto the scooter and hopped on behind him. "Come on!" With a mighty shove of her right foot, she pushed off.

"At least put on a helmet!" Emily called after her. But Rani didn't seem to hear. She sailed down the aisle and then swooped right and headed into housewares.

Trailing Rani and Jonah, Emily skidded around the corner and caught sight of a familiar figure among the blenders—Mrs. Pinkney. Penelope was by her side. Emily could see her smooth blond hair falling halfway down her back with the usual pink headband holding it tidily in place.

Emily hesitated. The best thing to do, she was sure, would be to deliver Jonah to Mrs. Pinkney at once. That would hopefully get Rani off the scooter.

But it would also mean calling Mrs. Pinkney's attention to the fact that Rani was *on* a scooter . . . and Emily didn't think that was a good idea at all.

Before she could figure out what to do, she saw Jonah lift one hand off of the handlebars and point to his mother.

Rani wove between shopping carts and dodged a tall, skinny man lugging a tall, skinny wastebasket. He spun as they scooted past and staggered into the arms of a lady carrying a copper saucepan on top of a fluffy white pillow. Emily ducked around them.

Rani swept in an arc around Mrs. Pinkney and Penelope, slid to a halt, and dropped Jonah off at his mother's feet. Then she pushed off once more and shouted, "Shoes ahoy!" in a ringing voice as she went rocketing down the aisle.

Emily charged past the Pinkneys. She heard Jonah whisper, "Wow," but the faint word was all but drowned out by Rani's whoop as she swung the cart around a corner, then another. She balanced on her left foot and stretched her right leg behind her like a figure skater gliding over the ice. Her pajama pants rippled in the breeze and she headed straight at the towering display of shoeboxes.

Emily didn't want to watch what happened next, but she couldn't look away.

At the last moment, Rani avoided slamming into the tower. She swung a neat circle all the way around the shoeboxes and headed back for Emily. She seemed to be slowing down.

Emily slowed down too. Her knees felt rubbery with relief. Rani hadn't knocked down the tower of shoeboxes, after all. They could just get the scooter back where it belonged and everything would be—

But instead of stopping, Rani orbited Emily and shoved off even harder than before. She zoomed back down the aisle, heading straight at the tower once again.

Emily sped up.

A despairing voice came from behind her. "Young ladies! Young ladies!" It was Hello-My-Name-Is-Blur.

"Rani! Get off! You can't keep riding that scooter!" Emily shrieked at Rani's back.

Wide-eyed but obedient, Rani hopped off. Emily, gasping for breath, staggered to her side.

"What else am I supposed to do with it?" Rani asked.

Although Rani had gotten off as directed, she hadn't stopped the scooter. It trundled on its way and plowed into the tower of shoeboxes.

CHAPTER 13

Emily stifled a wail as the scooter toppled over onto its side.

The tower wobbled. Hello-My-Name-Is-Blur dove past Rani and Emily, hurdled the fallen scooter, and flung himself at the tower with outstretched arms. He hugged it as if it were a long-lost relative.

Emily let out her breath slowly.

A single box fell from the very top. It bounced off Hello-My-Name-Is-Blur's bald head and hit the floor at Rani's feet. The lid popped off.

Rani peered inside. The box was empty.

"Oh. We need some boxes with shoes inside them, please," she informed Hello-My-Name-Is-Blur.

"Young lady!" He dropped his arms from the tower and turned to face Rani.

Emily felt herself begin to shrivel inside. Rani had gotten away with the popcorn and the caramels and the vacuum cleaner. But this? She was not going to get away with this.

She would get in trouble. They would *both* get in trouble.

How could Rani be so happy? So helpful? And such a disaster at the same time?

Hello-My-Name-Is-Blur stared down at them. Behind his back, the tower, released from his embrace, began to sway again. "I don't think you realize—What were you thinking—*Where* is your mother?"

"In Patagonia," Rani told him.

"Watch out!" Emily cried.

Rani hopped backward, snagging Emily by the arm, as four more shoeboxes rained down around Hello-My-Name-Is-Blur.

"No!" he cried in despair. He spun back around and flung himself at the tower so hard that he knocked the entire thing over.

Emily liked her new shoes very much. They were bright red and each one had a shiny gold zipper up one side. Rani had paid for them with a wad of cash she'd pulled from a zippered compartment deep inside her backpack.

She was wearing them as she sat next to Rani at the bus stop outside of the SuperSmartSaverMart. "My dad will pay you back for the shoes as soon as he gets here," she told Rani.

Where *was* her dad, anyway? Shouldn't he have gotten to the store by now?

"Oh, that's okay," Rani said. "It was nice of them to find shoes in your size so quickly."

Emily sighed. Explaining this, she thought, might take a while.

"Rani," she began. "They weren't actually being nice. They just wanted us to leave."

Rani hadn't meant to do anything wrong. Emily knew that. Rani honestly had no idea she'd even *done* anything wrong.

If they were going to be friends, Emily was going to have to explain things to her. To explain *everything* to her.

"I kept telling you," she said as patiently as she could. "You can't take things without paying for them."

"But I *did* pay for things!" Rani protested.

Well, that was true. Rani had paid for the popcorn. And the caramels. And the pinwheel. And the shoes that Emily was wearing right now.

"Well, okay," Emily agreed. "But the vacuum cleaner . . ."

"Elsie's mom paid for that," Rani pointed out.

True again.

"And the scooter . . ."

"Wasn't that fun?" Rani grinned.

"All those shoeboxes."

"It was a shame that worker knocked them down. It's funny they didn't want us to pick them back up. But I don't think they really wanted us to leave. That can't be right. Everyone was so friendly. Like that clown—there he is! Rich! Hello, Rich! It's us!" Rani waved wildly.

Emily looked around, but she didn't see anybody in a clown costume. The man Rani was waving at was dressed in perfectly ordinary jeans and a shabby gray sweatshirt. He walked around a corner of the SuperSmartSaverMart building and vanished from their sight.

"He didn't hear me. I'll go find him." Rani jumped up.

"No, Rani! We have to wait—" Emily's next words were cut off by the rumbling and wheezing of a bus that pulled up alongside the curb. Her father jumped out. "Girls, I am so sorry I'm late. The bus took forever and then there was an accident on the highway and we had to take a detour and got stuck behind a dump trunk and I—Is that your new friend Rani? Where's she going?"

Emily caught a glimpse of Rani's orange T-shirt as she vanished around a corner of the SuperSmartSaverMart.

"I think Rani went to find a clown," she told her father.

Together, Emily and her father followed Rani. They found her talking to the man in the gray sweatshirt. Without his clown costume and makeup, he looked like any other person—probably a bit older than high school but not as old as Emily's parents. Somewhere in between.

"Sure I remember you," he was saying as Emily ran up

to join them. Her father hurried along behind. "You're the one who asked my name. Nobody ever does that."

Rani was craning her neck and leaning to one side to stare at something behind Rich.

"Wow, this is the best part of the store!" she said.

Rich seemed as confused as Emily felt. "Back here?"

Dumpsters lined the wall of the SuperSmartSaverMart. Many had their lids propped open by all the stuff inside.

"It's just trash pickup and employee parking," Rich said. "Hey, I don't think you should climb on that!"

Rani had clambered up one side of a dumpster and was peering in.

"Oh, check this out!" she exclaimed.

Emily could see bright plastic sleds and snow shovels sticking out of the trash bin. A giant inflatable snowman was draped over one side, looking gloomy despite his jaunty hat.

"That's just winter stuff the store can't sell," Rich said. "The manufacturer didn't want it back, so they're throwing it all away."

"Rani, get down from there!" Emily's father said in what Emily thought of as his teacher voice.

Rani dropped off the side of the dumpster, but she didn't look at Emily's father. Her eyes were on Rich.

"Throwing it all away?" she asked breathlessly, as if it were too good to be true.

"Yeah." Rich shrugged. "Huge waste, but . . ."

Rani clapped her hands. "I love your store!" she exclaimed. "You really *do* want people to have anything they want!"

CHAPTER 14

A little later, Emily lay on her bed, staring at Rani's purple balloon bobbing gently against her ceiling.

Once they'd gotten home from the SuperSmart-SaverMart, she'd found it still tied to her belt loop. In all the excitement, she'd completely forgotten to take it off and give it back to Rani.

There was a whirring sound from overhead. Then a *bam!* And another *bam!*

Emily sat up.

Was Rani building something new? What would it be? At this point, Emily felt that nothing from a roller-skating rink to an aquarium full of jellyfish could surprise her very much.

Should she go upstairs and find out?

Emily got out of bed. Whatever Rani was doing up there, it was sure to be astonishing. Spectacular. Incredible.

Then Emily hesitated and sank back down on her mattress. Because sometimes, maybe, you could have a little too much astonishing, spectacular, incredible.

It was hard to believe that she'd only met Rani five days ago. Five days—less than a week.

Whirr came the noise from overhead. And then a brisk *rap rap rap.*

But all that noise didn't mean that Emily *had* to go up and see what Rani was doing. She could just flop back on her bed and admire her new shoes and relax.

Except that she was starting to get a little curious. . . .

Bam! Bam, bam, bam!

Those weren't hammer blows from overhead, Emily realized. That sound came from knuckles rapping on her own front door.

Emily heard that door open. "Oh, hello, Janice," her dad said.

Janice? Who was Janice?

"Come on in," Emily's dad said next.

"No, thank you. I can't stay. I simply thought you should be aware . . ."

Mrs. Pinkney. Janice was Mrs. Pinkney. Mrs. Pinkney was talking to Emily's dad.

Before she thought, Emily was across her bedroom, huddled against the door and listening as hard as she could.

"I'm not upset," Mrs. Pinkney was saying. "Not angry. Please don't think I'm angry."

"Well, of course," Emily's dad said.

"But concerned. Yes. Very concerned," Mrs. Pinkney went on. "I will need to go upstairs and talk to that child's parents. Naturally. But before I do . . ."

The vacuum cleaner. The scooter. Shoeboxes raining down. Mrs. Pinkney was telling Emily's dad everything that had taken place at the SuperSmartSaverMart.

And then she was going to go upstairs and tell Rani's parents. Except, of course, that there wouldn't be any parents upstairs for her to tell.

Emily had to do something.

She and Rani were friends, right? Rani had said so.

Emily had a feeling that it was going to turn out to be a lot of work, having Rani as a friend. But even so, Emily couldn't let Mrs. Pinkney find out that Rani lived all alone in an attic and slept in a hammock and had a big black dog who looked after her.

How was Emily going to warn Rani, though? There was no way Emily could run upstairs. Her dad and Mrs. Pinkney stood in the doorway, talking and talking and talking.

Emily's gaze traveled to the window of her bedroom.

If she were Rani, she could throw on a climbing harness and scale the wall up to the fourth floor. But she didn't have a harness. And she wasn't Rani.

Could something else go up that way, maybe? Something that wasn't Emily?

Emily leaped to her desk and grabbed a scrap of paper and a pen. She scribbled a quick message on the paper.

Don't open the door.

Then she snatched the string of Rani's balloon and tied the message to it. She rushed to her window and flung it open.

"Rani!" she called as loudly as she dared—which wasn't very loud. "Rani!"

Surely Rani would not hear her over the *rasp rasp rasp* of what sounded like a saw biting deep into wood. But miraculously, the attic window right above Emily's inched open.

A black muzzle poked out.

"Otto," Emily whispered. "Catch!" She let the string of the balloon go.

It was a silly thing to do. Emily knew it the moment the balloon drifted out of her reach. It was the kind of thing Rani might do, expecting a dog to catch a balloon . . . but she was Emily, not Rani.

The purple balloon floated up to the window. Otto didn't move.

How could Emily have been so stupid?

The dangling string was now in front of Otto's nose. Delicately, he nipped at it. Then he drew his head back inside the window. The balloon went with him. Emily's father knocked on her door.

He opened it without waiting for an answer.

"Emily," he said. "What exactly happened at the store this afternoon? Riding scooters around the aisles? Playing with vacuum cleaners? Knocking down half the shoe department?"

Emily turned away from the window. "I wasn't riding the scooter," she said to her dad. "Rani was. She didn't know she wasn't supposed to. And she was just using the vacuum to clean up."

"To clean up what?"

"The popcorn she spilled."

"She spilled popcorn?"

"But she paid for it. And she found Jonah Pinkney when he was lost!" she added. "I bet Mrs. Pinkney didn't tell you about that!"

Then Emily had to backtrack and explain everything that had taken place between Rani and Jonah.

"Well," Emily's father said when she was finished. "I think I should probably talk to Rani's mom."

"She's in Patagonia," Emily said, more or less automatically.

And then she wished she hadn't.

CHAPTER 15

After Emily told her dad where Rani's mom was, there was a lot more talking. In the middle of it, Emily's mom came home.

So then her dad talked to her mom. Her mom talked to Emily. All three of them went to talk to Mr. Armand, who was out back feeding the chickens.

There was a new contraption inside their pen, a whirligig of shiny metal and fluttering flags. Mr. Armand was pouring a cupful of grain into a funnel. The seeds trickled down a metal chute and spilled into a circular tray. Red flags spread out to catch the breeze and the tray slowly revolved.

The chickens came over to inspect their dinner.

"Patagonia, yes," Mr. Armand agreed. "Rani's mother asked if Rani could stay in the attic. All fine."

Emily watched Araminta, Betty, and Carlotta nibble their rotating meal. The spinning tray had a little mirror propped up on it. Araminta pecked at her own reflection each time it went past.

"Did Rani build that?" she asked.

Mr. Armand nodded. But Emily's mother wasn't interested in chicken feeders.

"She's only a child!" Emily's mom said. "Living all alone in that attic? She's a little girl!"

Mr. Armand stroked Carlotta's feathery head.

"A little girl, yes. But not an ordinary little girl," he said. "I met her first when she was three months old. Even then, I could tell. I assure you, Mrs. Robbins, Rani is as safe in that attic as she would be inside a fortress. All is most assuredly fine."

Emily watched the chickens eat as the grown-ups talked and talked and talked. Finally Emily's mother threw up both hands.

"School, then," she said. "At least she has to go to school."

Mr. Armand nudged Carlotta forward to be sure she got her fair share of dinner.

"School," he said thoughtfully. "Yes. I can see that school would be important. Very well. I will talk to Rani. Tomorrow she will go to school."

Emily woke up on Friday morning feeling a flutter deep inside that was half nervousness and half excitement. Last evening her mom had spent a lot of time on the phone, and everything had been arranged. Rani would come with Emily to the Henrietta Minnow School.

Emily changed into her school clothes and pulled on the new red shoes just before her mom opened the door.

"Oh, good, you're up," she said. "Go get Rani and tell her to come down here for breakfast. At least we can be sure that poor child gets a decent meal!"

Emily thought that "poor child" was not exactly the way she'd describe Rani. But she was glad of an excuse to run up to the attic. She needed to talk to Rani before the school day started.

When she knocked on Rani's door, there was no answer. But surely she was there. Where else would she be?

"Rani!" she called. "It's me! Open up!"

Rani's voice drifted out from inside the attic. "Oh! Are we done playing Don't Open the Door?"

Emily sighed.

"Yes, we're done!" she told Rani. "Hurry up!"

The door swung open. Emily took one step inside and stopped.

There was a trampoline. It was made of stretchy white material and near the center was a squashed face with a long, thin, orange nose and a flattened top hat.

"The snowman!" she said. "From the dumpster! Rani, you went back and took the snowman?"

"Sure thing," Rani answered. "Rich helped me."

Rani had spread out the fabric of what had once been an inflatable snowman and fastened long, thick springs all around its edges. Ropes stretched from the springs to the walls. She tightened up a carabiner attaching one of the ropes to the hook holding it taut.

"Try it out!" she said. "I need a test subject."

Emily took another step into the room. "You want me to be your guinea pig?"

"Don't be silly. A guinea pig wouldn't enjoy a trampoline at all. Come on!"

CHAPTER 16

Emily knew that her parents were waiting with breakfast downstairs . . . but surely a few jumps wouldn't take that long.

She climbed onto the trampoline, bent her knees, and pushed off. Her hair lifted slightly and then whooshed back down over her shoulders when she landed.

Rani took a turn and did her best to touch the ceiling with her outstretched fingers. Today she had on a purple blouse with a floppy collar, and she'd tied a bright orange scarf around her waist. Her pink skirt swirled with each jump, allowing Emily a glimpse of the frilly, knee-length, lime-green pantaloons Rani had on underneath.

Then Emily jumped again, higher than before. Dust

motes swirled around her, golden in the light from the tall windows.

But breakfast and school were waiting. Emily flopped down onto the stretchy material. It quivered under her and then steadied.

“Listen, Rani,” she said.

“Yes?” Rani was tightening one of the ropes. “Higher. We definitely need to go higher.”

“Really, Rani, you have to listen,” Emily insisted. “Mrs. Pinkney was at our apartment. She wanted to come up here and talk to your mom.”

“Oh.” Rani gave the rope a final tug. “She would have been disappointed, because my mom’s—”

“In Patagonia. I know! But, Rani, you can’t tell Mrs. Pinkney that.”

Emily’s parents already knew that Rani was living by herself in the attic. But Mrs. Pinkney didn’t. And Emily was positive that she had better not find out.

“She’s not going to understand,” Emily told Rani.

“I could show her Patagonia on a map,” Rani offered.

“No!” Emily groaned. “Rani, just trust me, please. Don’t

tell Mrs. Pinkney your mom's not here. You're coming to school with me, and Penelope Pinkney's in my class. You've met Penelope, right?"

Rani nodded. "She says dogs are unsanitary."

Emily refused to be distracted by the topic of Penelope and dogs. "Just don't talk about Patagonia at school, okay? Or Penelope will tell *her* mom all about *your* mom for sure."

Rani's forehead wrinkled. "But I don't see why Mrs. Pinkney should miss my mother so much. I'm the one who misses her. Mrs. Pinkney doesn't even know her."

Emily blinked.

"Rani, you miss your mom?" she asked.

It sounded like such a silly question. But Rani was always so cheerful. She never seemed worried or lonely or scared. So Emily hadn't thought about how it must feel to be Rani, up in the attic with just Otto for company.

"Of course I do," said Rani.

Emily listened to the quiet that filled up the attic. And she began to understand that, even though Rani was the most unusual person Emily had ever met, she was still a kid. A kid who missed her mom.

"Anyway," Emily said after the quiet had gone on long enough. "My mom says you should come downstairs for breakfast. It's probably oatmeal."

"Oatmeal!" Rani's wide grin lit up her face. "I love oatmeal!"

Rani insisted that oatmeal was best with honey, raisins, chocolate chips, and frozen peas. Emily found most of these things in the cupboards or in the freezer.

When she shut the freezer door and turned around with the bag of peas in her hand, she saw Otto nudge open a drawer with his nose and reach inside to pick up a bunch of napkins between his teeth. He walked over to the kitchen table and laid a napkin at each place.

Emily hadn't even realized that Otto had come downstairs with them. He could be very quiet for such a big dog.

Her father seemed startled to see Otto as well. He stood holding a travel mug of coffee in one hand and a pile of math papers in the other.

"How did you train him to do that?" he asked, staring at the dog.

Rani shrugged. "I didn't. He just has very strict ideas about etiquette."

"Eat your breakfast, girls!" Emily's mother had poked her head in the kitchen door. "Rani, are you all set for lunch?" Rani nodded as Emily's mom rubbed her eyes. "Let's go, shake a tail feather, has anyone seen my good black shoes?" She caught sight of Otto and sneezed.

"Allergies," Emily explained to Rani.

Otto was sent back upstairs with his own bowl of oatmeal. Rani found the good black shoes under the sofa. Emily's dad left while Emily and Rani were finishing their breakfasts. They gulped down the last mouthful just as it was time to go.

"Shake a tail feather!" Rani bellowed, and she was off down the stairs with her red backpack bouncing on her shoulders.

Emily scurried to catch up.

Her friend was going to need a lot of help at the Henrietta Minnow School. Emily knew that she couldn't let her guard down for a minute. No matter what happened, she'd have to stick close to Rani all day long.

CHAPTER 17

When they reached school, Rani started to climb the wall around the playground again, but Emily snagged the orange scarf around her waist and tugged her back down. She and Rani walked around to the gates and entered the playground just like everyone else.

The bell rang. Kids swept inside as teachers called out reminders to walk, to form lines, to head straight to classrooms. "I'll take you both in," Emily's mother said as she caught up to them.

"Are you coming to school too?" Rani asked.

"Well, no."

"Isn't there anything you need to learn?"

Emily's mom smiled. "Quite a lot, actually. But right now I

just have to talk to the office." She led the way through the front door. Rani skipped behind. Her silver shoes twinkled in the gloom of the hallway.

Emily caught hold of Rani's arm. "You have to walk," she told her.

"Sure thing!" Rani flipped over to walk on her hands. Her pink skirt fell over her face. Her legs in their lime-green pantaloons waved in the air.

Kids on their way to classrooms turned to stare.

"On your feet! Walk on your feet!" Emily cried out, but Rani had moved quite a way down the hallway. She didn't seem to hear.

Emily's mom had already gone into the office. Rani followed through the open door. Emily got there in time to see Rani flip over into a neat backbend and come up on her feet right in front of the principal's desk.

Her skirt settled down over her knees as Mr. Cleary looked up from his computer. He shook hands with Emily's mother and they talked over what had already been decided—that Rani could come along to Emily's class for the day.

"As a prospective student," Mr. Cleary said. "To see how everything . . ." He paused. "Suits."

Rani nodded happily. "What kind of a suit? A bathing suit?" She began to rummage in her backpack.

Emily snagged her hand. "No suit. Come on, Rani. Let's go."

On Fridays, Emily's class went to the library for first period. Since they'd missed attendance and morning meeting while in the office, Emily took Rani straight there.

Rani paused in the doorway with wide eyes.

"Wow," she whispered.

Emily glanced from side to side. She saw the shelves of books, the fuzzy orange rug where her class was already gathered, the reading corner with the three beanbag chairs, and the display of books on insects with the poster that read WHAT'S BUGGING YOU?

She liked the library, but it had never struck her as so amazing that she'd need to stand in the doorway and stare.

"Over here," Emily told Rani. She hurried toward the rug. "Sit by me."

But there was no answer. "Rani!"

Emily spotted Rani's silver shoes in the reading corner. The rest of Rani lay on her back in a beanbag chair. She'd snagged a book off one of the shelves, but she didn't seem to be reading it. It was open over her face, as if she were trying to block her eyes from the light.

"Who's *that*?" Anson Crutcher asked. He was twisting around on the rug to get a good look at Rani.

"My new neighbor," Emily told him. She raised her voice a little—just a little, because it was the library, after all. "Rani!"

Rani didn't stir. Had she fallen asleep? Could anybody fall asleep that suddenly?

"She's weird," Anson said. There was admiration in his voice.

"She's *very* weird," Penelope Pinkney said with no admiration in her voice at all. She was sitting directly across from Anson. Penelope usually made it a point to sit as far away from Anson as possible.

Emily started toward the reading corner, but just then Ms. Moreno, the librarian, got up from the chair behind her desk. Emily hesitated and then slowly sank down on the rug beside Anson. Her whole body felt tight and hot. Would Rani get in trouble before first period even began?

"Good morning, everyone," Ms. Moreno said.

Emily liked Ms. Moreno. She smiled a lot and had glossy black hair that she usually wore up in a bun on the back of her head, and she kept a bowl of peppermints on the desk next to the slot for returned books. Emily did not want Ms. Moreno to get annoyed at Rani before she even got to know her.

The kids who were fidgeting or talking or wiggling into comfortable positions settled down. Maureen Kenilworth, who'd flopped onto her back to study the ceiling tiles, sat up.

Rani didn't stir.

"The office just let me know that we have a prospective student here today," Ms. Moreno went on. "So let's all—hmmmm. Where is she?"

Penelope's arm snapped out to point at Rani.

"Ah." Ms. Moreno's eyebrows went up. She studied a note in her hand. "Excuse me. Rani? Is that your name?"

"What kind of name is that?" Penelope whispered, loud enough for the kids around her to hear but too quiet for Ms. Moreno to notice.

The librarian went on. "What are you doing with that book, Rani?"

"Experimenting." Rani's voice came from underneath the book still propped over her face.

"Experimenting how?"

"With the words. To see if they'll soak right into my brain."

"I see." Ms. Moreno's mouth twitched slightly.

"I think it's working," Rani went on.

"Well. Could you come and take a seat for now and continue your experimentation at home, please?"

"Sure thing!" Rani hopped up, tossed her book into the beanbag chair, sashayed around a fern in a pot, paused to plant a loud, smacking kiss on the glass of the fish tank, turned a cartwheel, and ended up next to the rocking chair on the orange rug.

"Where would you like me to take this seat?" she asked Ms. Moreno.

Ms. Moreno's eyes had gotten very wide. "I would just like you to sit on the rug," she said slowly.

Rani plopped down on the rug and sat bolt upright. With her eyes clamped tightly shut, she lifted both hands to her head and squeezed as if she were trying to hold it together.

"Rani? Are you all right?" Ms. Moreno asked. She sounded alarmed.

"I can still feel all those words settling in," Rani announced.

"Oh." Ms. Moreno took her own seat in the rocking chair. "Well, everyone—"

Rani's eyes popped open and she took her hands down from her head. "All in!" she announced.

Emily glanced around.

Almost everyone in the class had their eyes fixed on Rani. There were giggles and whispers. Penelope's mouth was slightly open, but when she caught Emily's gaze, she turned her face away and seemed to become deeply fascinated by the insect book display.

"*Weird!*" Anson murmured with delight.

Clearly, Emily would have to do a better job of explaining the rules to Rani.

CHAPTER 18

Ms. Moreno cleared her throat. "I hope everyone was able to finish the chapters of *Hatchet* you were reading at home. Someone tell me what's been happening to Brian."

Penelope's hand shot into the air. "He went fishing," she said.

"So now he's going to be okay," Dylan Okoshi put in. "He can get food whenever he needs it."

Anson shook his head. "He can't just be *okay*," he objected. "There's still, like, half the book to go. That'd be really boring if he was just *okay* now."

"Let's find out, shall we?" Ms. Moreno opened the book. "This next part gives us some real clues about what the author's message is. 'Mistakes,'" she read aloud. "'Small mistakes could turn into disasters.'"

Emily was so busy thinking about how true that was that she missed the next several paragraphs.

Rani, however, didn't.

"It's definitely true about skunks," she whispered to Emily. "They're not as cute as people think!"

Emily made a shushing motion with her hand.

"Skunks aren't afraid of anything. They're kind of—"

Ms. Moreno stopped reading. "Emily and Rani," she said. "Save the conversation for later, please."

Emily winced. She hated it when teachers acted as if being talked to was the same as talking.

"Because once my mom and I went canoeing on the Allagash River and there was this skunk," Rani went on. "You wouldn't believe it if I told you about the skunk. But hippos are worse. They're territorial, see, and they don't want anybody else in their part of the river. So—"

"Rani." Ms. Moreno's voice was a little firmer than before. "Unless this is something the whole class needs to know, please settle down."

"Sure!" Rani jumped up eagerly. "Everyone should hear this, because if you encounter an angry hippo, it's really important to know what to do. They're way more fierce than they look. They don't smile. You know how in picture books they're always smiling? But in real life they don't. And they're much faster than you think." She took a step into the middle of the rug, slowing turning so that she could talk to the entire circle of kids around her. "You're not going to be able to outrun one, so don't try. And diving in the river to escape is a really bad idea, because hippos can swim."

Rani paused to make motions with both arms as if she were doing the breaststroke through a murky river. Ms. Moreno seized the chance to speak up.

"Rani, this is supposed to be story time," she said a little weakly.

Rani nodded. "I know. This is a really good story I'm telling. Once I was having a picnic by a river and a hippo charged right out of the water. I figured he was going to trample all over my peanut butter sandwiches, and I'd put a lot of honey on them, so I didn't want to lose them. What I did was—"

"Rani!" Ms. Moreno broke in.

"Yes?" Rani turned to her. "Do you like peanut butter and honey sandwiches too?"

Ms. Moreno took in a slow breath.

"Story time means that I read the story," she said. "The students sit on the rug. And listen."

"Oh." Rani plopped down on the rug next to Emily. "But it's probably lucky for that kid Brian in the book that he only had a skunk to worry about," she added. "Instead of a hippo."

Ms. Moreno lifted the book from her lap. Anson leaned over Emily and poked Rani in the arm.

"What did you do about the hippo? And the sandwiches?" he whispered.

"Shhh!" Rani told him, her eyes on Ms. Moreno. "Story time. Anyway, hippos don't like peanut butter."

Ms. Moreno raised her voice a little as she started to read again, but Emily wasn't sure anyone was really listening. Kids murmured and whispered and stared at Rani. Anson kept shaking his head. "They don't like peanut butter?" he muttered. "What *do* they like?"

Emily tried to pay attention. But in her imagination, huge

gray hippos thundered through the Canadian pinewoods, spitting out peanut butter sandwiches and grumbling because they wanted egg salad.

It was a relief when Ms. Moreno snapped the book closed and told the class they could choose their own books to take home. Emily hopped up from the rug and showed Rani around the shelves. "You can pick any book you want," she explained.

Rani considered a giant dictionary with a gleam in her eye. Emily shook her head and pulled one of her own favorites off the shelf—*Binny for Short*. "You'll like it. It has a dog in it." She pushed the book into Rani's hands.

"Checkout time!" Ms. Moreno called.

They lined up by the librarian's desk, books in hand. Anson leaned past Annie Park to tap Rani on the shoulder. "Hey, you never said—" he began.

But by that time, Rani and Emily were at the front of the line. Ms. Moreno smiled at them as she scanned their books.

Rani beamed back. "Whose turn will it be to tell the story next time?" she asked eagerly.

Ms. Moreno frowned, a little confused. "Well, it's . . . my turn usually."

Rani looked puzzled. "Doesn't anyone else have any good stories? I have lots! One time—"

"Come on, Rani." Emily tugged Rani back toward the library door.

"Hey, I want to know—" Anson started to say.

"Anson, your book, please?" Ms. Moreno asked him.

When the whole fourth grade was lined up at the door, Ms. Moreno came to lead them down the hall. As they passed the school entrance, Rani swerved while everyone else went straight on.

Emily snagged Rani's arm and pulled her back in line. "Where are you going?" she whispered.

"Home. Aren't you coming?"

"No!" The two of them had slowed down, creating a gap in the line. Emily scurried to catch up. "You can't go home now, Rani. There's lots of school left."

"There is?" Rani blinked in astonishment. "My brain feels very full. All those words, you know. Are you sure that isn't enough education for one day?"

"No! We've got math next. And science. And then there's lunch."

Ahead of them in line, Anson spun around. "But what do the *hippos* eat for lunch?" he bellowed.

Rani gazed at him in mild surprise. "River weeds, of course."

Anson stared at her. "That's it?"

"Of course not," Rani told him. "They like pickles to go with them."

CHAPTER 19

Emily managed to get Rani down the hall and into their classroom without much more difficulty. Rani seemed to like math. And during science she was so interested in watching dry ice change from a solid to a gas with no liquid state in between that she mostly stayed in her seat.

Emily began to hope that Rani might actually make it through the rest of the school day.

Then lunchtime arrived. In the cafeteria, the fourth graders found seats at their long table. But not Rani. She slipped away to a window, opened it, and whistled through the gap between her teeth, loudly enough that heads turned all around.

Emily gestured frantically. What was Rani doing?

At the table, kids slapped down trays or flipped open lunch boxes or dug into sacks to pull out food. Rani came to sit beside Emily empty-handed.

"Rani, you said you had lunch," Emily said.

"No, I didn't," Rani answered calmly.

Emily thought back to that morning in her kitchen. Her mom had asked Rani if she had a lunch. . . . No, her mom had asked Rani if she was *all set* for lunch. Wasn't that the same thing, though?

Maybe she should tell Rani to get in line to buy lunch. Or it might be simpler just to share. She ripped her almond butter sandwich into halves and offered one to Rani. "Here," she said.

"Thanks!" Rani gave her a bright smile. "But I'm fine. I'm just waiting."

"Waiting for what?" Anson asked from the other side of the table.

"Delivery," Rani answered.

Emily turned toward the open window. Otto was outside, his front paws up on the sill. A polka-dot lunch sack hung from his jaws.

Rani ran over to him. "Thanks!" she said cheerfully, taking the sack.

Emily hurried over to the window and tugged Rani back to the fourth-grade table before Mr. Cleary, who had lunch duty and who was talking to Ms. Moreno at the cafeteria door, could notice that they were both out of their seats.

"Ew." Penelope wrinkled her nose. "You let a dog carry your *lunch*? In its *mouth*?"

"Well, he needs his paws for walking," Rani answered.

Emily held her breath as Rani opened up her lunch sack, but there was nothing more unusual inside than a plum and a chunk of pita bread stuffed with lettuce and hummus. Rani took a huge bite and chewed while answering questions from all the fourth graders about Otto and how Rani had trained him to bring her lunch. Except for Penelope, who didn't say a word, although Emily noticed her glancing at Rani from time to time out of the corner of her eye. And except for Anson, who wanted to talk about hippos.

On the playground after lunch, he called to Rani from the tallest platform on the climber. Rani clambered nimbly up. Emily followed.

"What happened when the hippo charged out of the river?" Anson demanded.

Rani blinked at him. "What river?"

"The one you were having a picnic next to!" Anson bellowed. "With peanut butter sandwiches!"

Rani frowned.

"I've eaten peanut butter sandwiches by a *lot* of rivers," she said. "Peanut butter is good for you. Although it doesn't have as much protein as a tarantula. Insects are very nutritious. Arachnids too, of course."

Just then Penelope's head appeared over the edge of the platform. "What are you talking about up here?" she asked suspiciously.

"Eating tarantulas," Anson said.

Penelope made a face, but she climbed the rest of the way up the ladder and sat down cross-legged between Rani and Emily. "That's gross. That's unsanitary."

Anson rolled his eyes. "Then go away if you don't like what we're talking about."

"You can't exclude people. Excluding is mean." Penelope smoothed the skirt of her brown jumper over her knees.

"Excluding?" Rani echoed.

"You have to let everybody play all the time," Emily explained to Rani. "There's a rule."

"Oh." Rani grinned. "That's great! Otherwise we'd be like the orangutans and keep people out of the tea parties."

Penelope's face wrinkled. "Orangutans don't—"

Rani whipped off the orange scarf around her waist. "How about Capture the Flag?" she asked.

Emily and Anson exchanged a glance. There were quite a few games that weren't allowed on the playground of the Henrietta Minnow School. Was Capture the Flag one of them? Emily wasn't sure. Anson didn't seem sure either.

Before they could decide, Rani leaned forward to stuff her orange scarf down the back of Penelope's dress.

"Penelope's got the flag!" she sang out. "Capture her! Ten-second head start!"

Penelope made one squirming attempt to yank the scarf out, but she couldn't reach it. Looking alarmed, she turned and fled down the ladder.

"One . . . two . . . three . . ." Rani shouted.

"Rani!" Emily grabbed at her friend's arm. "Mrs. Pinkney is *Penelope's mom*. Remember?"

Rani nodded happily. "Sure! Four . . . five . . . six . . ."

On the ground, a group of kids had gathered. Penelope was squeaking, "I don't want to play! I don't want the stupid flag!" as she twisted around, trying to remove Rani's scarf from the back of her jumper.

"You're not supposed to say *stupid*," Annie Park told her. "I'm on Rani's team!"

"Seven-eight-nine-ten!" Rani shouted. She brushed Emily's hand off her arm and vaulted to the ground, landing in front of Penelope.

"You have to let us play with you, right?" Rani asked. "Isn't that the rule?"

Penelope stared at Rani in utter confusion. Then she began to run, with Rani close behind.

Emily was still making her way down from the climber. She was pretty sure this was all going to be against a rule. And no matter what, it was important to keep Rani as far away as possible from Penelope.

She jumped the last few feet and had just landed when the orange scarf slipped out of the back of Penelope's dress and fell to the wood chips.

Emily sighed with relief.

Rani snatched the scarf up.

"Capture me!" she crowed, and scrambled up the nearest slide.

CHAPTER 20

Frantic thoughts swirled inside Emily's brain. She had to catch Rani. She had to warn her about breaking rules . . . about upsetting Penelope . . . about everything!

There was a rule about not going up a slide, but Emily found herself tearing on hands and knees after Rani. Anson was just behind her.

Rani leaped from the top of the slide with the scarf fluttering in her hand. Emily didn't dare jump, but she threw herself between Anson's legs and dove down the slide, trying to catch up.

Rani pelted across the swinging bridge with Emily on her heels. When Rani leaped over the railings, Emily wriggled under.

She was dimly aware of cries behind her. "Stop!" "That's not safe behavior!" "She made me be the flag!" The other kids chasing Rani—Anson and Annie, Samira and Gabriel, Maureen and Antonio—spread out like a comet's tail across the playground.

Somehow the closer Emily got to Rani, the less she was thinking about stopping her. Or warning her. Or making sure she followed every playground rule.

All of Emily's attention was now on the flag, flirting and fluttering so temptingly just beyond her reach. She was so close to grabbing it! Of all the kids chasing it, she was the first!

Rani's silver shoes flashed and the orange scarf danced. Emily lunged for it and felt it brush through her fingers. She slipped and rolled in the woodchips, ending up flat on her back, both arms flung out, laughing at the sky.

Rani was laughing too. High above Emily, she waved the orange scarf in long swoops through the air. "Can't capture me!" she sang. "Nobody can capture me!"

Rani looked so high up, Emily almost thought she might float away. It was something Rani would do. She'd rig a harness from a cloud or train a passing albatross to carry her in a sling. She'd soar into the sky, calling to everyone below to join her. . . .

"Rani! Get down from there!" Anson called.

Emily sat up. Her head swam for a moment and then cleared.

Rani was *not* floating through the sky. She was dancing

along the top of the playground wall, closer and closer to the gates.

"Rani, you have to get off the wall!" Emily called. "Now! Quick!"

She still wasn't sure if Capture the Flag was against the rules . . . but she knew that climbing the wall definitely was.

"Okay!" Rani called back.

She leaped off the wall . . . but she didn't land on the ground. Instead, somehow, she was clinging to the flagpole.

Hugging the slippery pole with her legs and arms, Rani shimmied upward. The orange scarf was clenched between her teeth.

"Is she going all the way to the top?" Anson asked. He was at Emily's shoulder.

Emily didn't know. She had the sense that a crowd had clustered behind them, but she worried that if she dared to glance away even for a moment, Rani was sure to fall.

Almost at the top by now, Rani let go of the pole with one hand and took the scarf from her mouth. Somehow she clipped the scarf to the pole just below the flag. A breeze lifted them both, and the orange swath of fabric rippled through the air along with the stars and stripes.

Rani slid down the flagpole and landed lightly on top of the wall. "Nobody will capture it now!" she declared.

That was when Mr. Cleary arrived, breathing heavily, his tie coming loose.

"Stay there!" he shouted at Rani.

Rani smiled at him.

"Everyone else keeps saying I should get down," she said. "And now you want me to stay up here. Which should I do?"

Mr. Cleary pointed a trembling finger at Rani. "Don't move," he said anxiously. "We're getting a ladder. Stay still!"

"Sure thing," Rani agreed. She seemed to take Mr. Cleary's instructions very seriously, because she planted both hands on her hips and froze, perfectly still.

She didn't stir so much as a finger until Mr. Hayes, the school custodian, shuffled over to the wall with a ladder on his shoulder. He propped the ladder up close to Rani's feet.

Then he climbed up himself, puffing a little.

"Now let's get you down," he said as his head came level with Rani's knees. He reached up a hand.

"Okay!" Rani said.

She shook Mr. Hayes's hand, jumped off the wall, landed at Mr. Cleary's feet, spread out her pink skirt, and took a bow.

Mr. Cleary let out a long, long breath.

"Rani? Please come with me to the office," he said.

Inside herself, Emily groaned.

CHAPTER 21

The rest of the fourth grade went back to their classrooms, minus Rani.

All the time they were practicing their cursive, Emily kept glancing at the door. But Rani didn't show up until they were halfway through a video on the American Revolution. She seemed like her usual self—not at all like a kid who had just gotten in trouble.

Emily didn't get a chance to find out what had happened in the office until after the bell rang for the end of the day. All the kids piled into the hallway and Emily grabbed Rani's arm.

"What did Mr. Cleary talk to you about?" she asked anxiously.

"A lot about rules," Rani answered. "Don't all these rules get in the way of the education?"

Maybe a little bit, Emily thought. But she didn't think she should say so.

"I could probably manage either the rules or the education," Rani went on thoughtfully. "But not both. Are there rules in this club too?"

Emily sighed. "Yes."

On Fridays after school Emily went to the Friendship and Feelings Club. That morning, her mother had arranged with Mr. Cleary for Rani to go too.

"Like about how to drink your tea?" Rani asked.

"No, other stuff. And Penelope goes to the club too. So, Rani, don't . . . I mean . . ." Emily struggled to find the right words. "Just try not to . . . do anything. You know. That Penelope will tell her mom about. Anything *more*. Please?"

Rani looked puzzled. But she nodded. "I'll try," she said.

Emily could tell that Rani meant it. But that didn't reassure her much.

They walked into the Friendship and Feelings room together. Emily went straight to the Feelings Chart. It hung on the wall beside the door.

On the chart were round circles with eyes and mouths—smiling, scowling, and everything in between. You were supposed to pick a circle showing how you felt today and move it beside your name.

Emily had to admit that she wasn't quite sure what she was feeling today. It had been worrying, keeping an eye on Rani all the time. But there had been the wild excitement of Capture the Flag. And the hippos during story time had been sort of fun too.

Anyway, she didn't really have to figure out how she was feeling, because Emily always picked the same face—the one where the mouth had a very slight curve for a smile. It meant you weren't as happy as the face with the big wide grin, but you weren't frowning (angry) or crying actual tears.

Most importantly, if you picked the slightly smiling face, Mr. Cleary would not make a point of coming to talk to you about how you were feeling that day. Mr. Cleary ran the Feelings and Friendship Club. From across the room, he smiled so widely that it looked a little fake to Emily.

"Rani! How lovely to see you again!" he exclaimed.

Mr. Cleary really liked the idea of a fresh start. He talked about it a lot, after somebody had broken a rule or cried or gotten mad. "Time for a fresh start!" he would say.

Emily guessed he was trying to show Rani that she was still having a fresh start after the Capture the Flag game and her visit to his office.

"Emily, have you explained to Rani how the Feelings Chart works?" Mr. Cleary went on.

"You take the face that matches your feelings and put it by your name," Emily mumbled. "There's one for guests. There."

Rani studied the chart, picked the face with the widest grin, and slapped it next to the GUEST label.

"Excellent! Excellent!" Mr. Cleary said. He swooped away to encourage all the kids to settle on the green rug.

Penelope eyed Rani from across the room. She marched over to the Feelings Chart, pulled off her own slightly smiling face with a rip of Velcro, and slapped a scowling face next to her name. Without a word she stomped over to sit on the rug.

The rest of the kids shuffled into a circle. Anson came in and forgot to visit the Feelings Chart in his hurry to grab a seat next to Rani.

"Can we play Capture the Flag again?" he whispered. "That was epic!"

Mr. Cleary sat down in his own place in the circle and clapped twice. All the kids who'd been paying attention clapped twice back at him. Emily got in on the second clap.

"Feelings Circle!" Mr. Cleary announced.

Emily glanced over at the Feelings Chart. Only Penelope's face had a frown on it. Everyone else knew better.

"Penelope, why don't you tell your friends what you're feeling?" Mr. Cleary asked. He bent forward a little encouragingly.

"Recess was just really, really hard for me," Penelope announced.

Emily let out a silent sigh and tugged at the gold zipper on one of her new shoes as Penelope explained how it had felt to be the flag in Capture the Flag. Beside her, Rani fidgeted.

"Aren't we going to *do* anything?" she whispered.

Emily shook her head. "We have to finish Feelings Circle first."

"Well, Penelope, an excellent job of sharing," Mr. Cleary said.

"I wasn't finished," said Penelope.

"Oh. I see." Even Mr. Cleary drooped a little. "Well, we want to have time for everyone, so—"

"Someone shouldn't make someone else be the flag if someone doesn't want to be the flag!" Penelope went on. "Because I think—no, I *feel*—"

Emily switched to the zipper on her other shoe.

Rani pulled one of her black curls to its full length and let it bounce back. Then another.

Anson was collecting old staples that had sunk into the fibers of the carpet. He showed them to Emily and Rani on his slightly grubby palm. Seventeen.

"Thank you, Penelope," said Mr. Cleary. "Very much."

"But I'm not—"

"We want to have time for everyone in the Feelings Circle, Penelope. Do you feel better now that you've shared? Would you like to change your face on the Feelings Chart?"

Penelope scowled. "No."

"Oh. Maybe later." Mr. Cleary turned to Penelope's neighbor with a smile. "Anabel?"

"Fine," said Anabel.

All the kids after Anabel said, "Fine" too. Or "Good" or "Okay." They'd all learned it was the quickest way to get the Feelings Circle over with.

Rani, however, had not learned this.

"And our new friend? Rani? How are you feeling?" Mr. Cleary asked. His smile stretched even wider.

CHAPTER 22

"Ebullient!" Rani sang out. She jumped to her feet. "I feel ecstatic, enthusiastic, exceptional!"

Rani did a handstand right in the center of the Feelings Circle. Her sneakers flashed.

"Feet on the floor, please!" Mr. Cleary cried out.

Rani arched her back and let her feet fall to the ground. In a full backbend, she looked up at Mr. Cleary with her hair bobbing around her face.

"What a good idea!" she said. "I feel even happier upside down."

Emily winced. She leaned forward, trying to catch Rani's eye. Didn't Rani remember she'd promised to try not to do anything odd? To follow all the rules?

But then, Rani probably thought she *was* following the rules. Feet on the floor was what Mr. Cleary had said—and that was where Rani's feet were.

"She's right!" Anson announced. His voice was a little muffled, because he was doing a headstand and his T-shirt had flopped down over his face. "It *does* feel better like this. Penelope should try it!"

"Friends, this is not the gymnasium!" Mr. Cleary called out. "There are no floor mats! Please, let's—"

Anson fell over. Emily had to dodge to avoid his feet. He sat up, red-faced and grinning.

Maybe, just maybe, Emily thought, it would be better if other kids were upside down too. Then Rani wouldn't be the only one to blame. Or the only one Mrs. Pinkney would hear about.

For that to work, it would need more than Rani and Anson.

Emily had never been able to do a headstand in her life. Or a handstand either. But Rani made it seem so easy. And Anson had fallen over, but he hadn't gotten hurt.

She got into a crouch and tucked her chin down into her chest. Wasn't that how you started? She rocked forward so that the top of her head was on the ground, her arms braced on the carpet.

She hesitated.

Did she feel happier like this? She wasn't sure. It felt cramped and dark and quiet, like being tucked up in a mousehole. And that was actually kind of nice.

She could smell the carpet, with its scent that was harsh and clean in a chemical way, and dusty too, and old. It smelled like all the kids' feet that had ever walked across it, the soles of their shoes sticky with dirt and spilled juice. And paint from the art room. Mud from the playground. Macaroni and cheese from the lunchroom. Chocolate milk too. Maybe a crunched pretzel or a bit of orange peel that had been trodden into the crannies of a sneaker.

Plus, Emily's feet were still on the floor. So she wasn't actually breaking a rule.

"Friends! Friends!" Mr. Cleary clapped desperately. "Let's come back to our Feelings Circle, please!"

A bit reluctantly, Emily came out of her crouch. She shook her head and blinked. Rani was still in her backbend. Two more kids had just fallen over. Maureen Kenilworth was draped face-up over a chair with her feet on one side and her head on the other.

Rani flipped upright. Maureen slithered off her chair. "Let's get started on our activity," Mr. Cleary said. He smiled as if he'd realized that he'd forgotten to do it for a while.

"Great! What are we doing?" Rani asked eagerly.

"Coloring," Emily told Rani. The activity was almost always coloring. She waved a hand at the table in the back of the room, where paper and crayons and markers had been laid out.

"Cool!" Rani charged toward the table. Emily followed more slowly.

"Can't we go outside?" Anson asked gloomily as he, too, headed for the table. He always asked this. He never got an answer.

"Express yourself!" Mr. Cleary told the club. He spread his arms wide and wiggled his fingers. "Express your feelings!"

Emily did not mind drawing, but she found it hard to do any kind of art when someone was telling her to express herself. It was much easier just to draw a picture than it was to decide if you were feeling orange or purple that day.

She settled in next to Rani. The only way she could imagine Rani expressing her feelings was by using fireworks or shooting stars. Would markers and crayons really be enough?

She glanced at Rani's paper. It was blank.

Rani was drawing on her hand instead. She had made a bracelet of intricate black lines going around her wrist.

"All done!" she announced. She smiled up at Mr. Cleary, who had come to stand behind her chair. "What's next?"

CHAPTER 23

"Next?" Mr. Cleary asked Rani. He frowned at her decorated hand.

"Our next activity?"

"There *is* no next activity," Mr. Cleary said. "This *is* what we are doing. Expressing our feelings. Through art."

"On these little bitty pieces of paper?" Rani sounded bewildered. "But aren't we a lot bigger than a piece of paper? I know! Let's put on a play!"

Mr. Cleary shook his head.

"In this club, we do not do anything that might make someone feel badly," he explained patiently. "Not everyone can have the lead role in a play. We don't want anyone to feel left out."

Rani cocked her head to one side, thinking this over. "Singing?" she suggested.

"Not everyone has the same talent when it comes to music."

"We could play soccer!" Rani suggested. "Or kickball!"

Anson brightened up. Mr. Cleary did not.

"Certainly not!" He was beginning to look a little panicked. "Do you know the statistics on childhood concussions? Now. Friends." He took a slow, careful breath. "We need to focus. And express our feelings. On *paper*."

For a moment Emily felt as if her own breath were stuck in her throat. Would Rani listen to Mr. Cleary?

What would happen if she didn't?

Everyone seemed to be wondering the same thing, including Mr. Cleary. They were all waiting for the next words to be spoken.

But the next words weren't Rani's. To Emily's surprise, they came from her own mouth.

"What about snack?" she asked.

Her voice felt faint and brittle. She thought no one would hear it. But because the room was so quiet, everyone did.

"Yes!" Mr. Cleary exclaimed. He sounded very relieved. "Snack! Certainly! Thank you, Emily, for the reminder. A healthy snack."

He hurried away to a closet on the other side of the room.

"Good idea!" Rani said to Emily. "I'm hungry. All the expressing and education really wears you out."

Emily had to agree.

Mr. Cleary was back with a tray. There were little paper cups on it, and each cup had exactly five pretzel sticks and three grapes.

Mr. Cleary moved down the table, handing each child a cup. Rani crunched her pretzels in a single bite. She tossed the grapes up into the air one by one and caught them in her mouth.

"I love grapes!" she said, and held out her cup to Mr. Cleary. "Any more?"

"Ah. No." Mr. Cleary frowned. "Portion control is very—"

"Oh, well, then." Rani stood up. "Thanks for the snack. Excuse me a moment."

She walked over to the window and opened it. She unlocked the screen and flung that up too.

"Safety! Please!" Mr. Cleary gasped as Rani grabbed both sides of the window frame and leaned out. She whistled, loud and shrill.

Mr. Cleary was at her side in a moment. "Rani, the window stays closed!" he said.

"Okay," said Rani. "I'll be sure to close it when I'm done."

Before Mr. Cleary could react, she hopped onto the windowsill and somersaulted off it.

Mr. Cleary yelped. Emily dashed over and peered out to see Rani picking herself out of a bush.

Just for a moment, Mr. Cleary's panic had made Emily forget that this classroom was on the first floor.

"Is she hurt?" Mr. Cleary gulped. "Tell her not to move. I'll go get the nurse. Nobody move!"

"She's fine," Emily told Mr. Cleary as Rani stood up, plucking leaves and twigs from her curls.

From outside the window, Rani reached up to the screen and tugged it down.

"You sound kind of worried," she said gently to Mr. Cleary. "I'm sure you can find a worried face for the Feelings Chart if you need it. Oh, there he is!"

Rani waved at Emily and ran to Otto, who was trotting serenely across the blacktop.

"Dog on the playground! Dog on the playground!" Mr. Cleary choked out. "Children, stay here. In this room. Oh my—"

He dashed to the door. They heard his shoes thumping down the hallway.

Anson was now at Emily's elbow. "What's she doing?" he asked eagerly.

Rani, with Otto by her side, had run over to the school gates and flung both wide open. On the other side, a white van was parked by the curb. The driver stuck an arm out of the van's window and waved to Rani.

Rani came jogging back to the classroom window. "Who wants ice cream?" she called.

"Me!" Anson shouted. He threw up the window screen and flung one leg over the sill.

CHAPTER 24

Later on, Emily tried to figure out how Rani had found the ice cream van so easily. Had it just been driving by? Had Otto somehow shown the driver where to go?

But at the moment, she and the rest of the Feelings and Friendship Club were not thinking of anything but ice cream.

As Anson teetered on the windowsill and the others crowded around to peer outside, only one person remained seated.

"We're supposed to stay in the room," Penelope said. She colored so hard that her crayon snapped in two.

Anson fell out of the window and into the bush.

"Yes," said Emily slowly. "We are."

Was that so important, really? If she took a second to think about it, Emily wasn't sure. What harm would it do to go onto the playground? They went out there every day.

Still, Emily couldn't help feeling a little sorry for Mr. Cleary. If he came back and found that the whole Feelings and Friendship Club had vanished, he'd be frantic.

"Rani?" Emily raised her voice a little. "Mr. Cleary told us to stay in here."

"Oh, he did? Okay. Come on, Anson, inside!" Rani boosted a bewildered, leafy Anson back through the window. He tumbled headfirst onto the carpet.

"What about the ice cream?" he demanded.

"Just wait!" Rani dashed toward the open gates where the white truck was idling. She said a few words to the driver. Then, to Emily's astonishment, the truck backed up a little, turned, and headed right through the open gates and into the schoolyard itself.

Anson whooped with delight.

The truck came slowly over the blacktop, scattering stray woodchips. Rani dashed ahead of it and hurtled in the window just before the truck swerved and came to a stop alongside the building.

The serving hatch in the side of the truck was even with the classroom window. It slid open and the driver stood behind it, wearing a white paper hat. Otto's nose popped into view under the driver's elbow.

"What can I get you?" he asked.

"A Mississippi mud bar!" Anson shouted.

"A cherry slushie!" Maureen Kenilworth chimed in.

"A bomb pop!"

"An Oreo snowstorm!"

"But we don't have any money," Emily said.

"You don't need any!" said Rani. "Everybody line up!"

When it was Emily's turn, she noticed that the server seemed familiar. "Rich?" she asked.

"Hey, there, Emily. What can I get you?"

"A hot fudge sundae?" Emily answered hesitantly. "How come you're not at the store?"

"Got a new job. Here you go!" He squirted whipped cream on the sundae until the frothy white tower began to wobble. Then he plonked on three cherries and handed it to her.

Emily took a bite. Whipped cream squished sweetly inside her mouth. The fudge was warm and the ice cream went from cold to cool to melting on her tongue.

"What about her?" Rich waved a dripping ice cream scoop at Penelope, who was still sitting at the table and coloring with what was left of her crayon. It had been worn down to a stub between her fingers.

"We *had* snack," she said, staring down at her paper. Her cheeks were so red they looked sore.

Rani bounced over to the table, holding a waffle cone in one hand. In it were three scoops of ice cream: bubble-gum, coffee chip, and rainbow sherbet. "But don't you want some ice cream too?" she asked Penelope.

"It's unsanitary. There's a *dog* in the truck. My mother wouldn't let me eat ice cream from a truck with a *dog* in it."

But Penelope's eyes had lifted from her paper.

"He's a very clean dog," Rani said encouragingly. "He licks himself every day. All over. Even—"

"Ewww!" Penelope made a face.

"There's nothing wrong with my sundae, Penelope," Emily said. "It's really good—see?"

Penelope glanced at the dark, satiny chocolate melting into the velvety white ice cream. The red cherries had made little pink hollows in the whipped cream.

Slowly, the corners of Penelope's mouth started to sag. Emily began to feel a little sorry for her.

She had always thought of Penelope as bossy. As grumpy. And now that Emily came to think about it, as a lot like her mother.

But now, for the first time, she found herself thinking of Penelope as unhappy. Because, really, how much fun could it be, being Penelope Pinkney every single day?

"Do you want a bite?" she asked.

CHAPTER 25

Still staring at Emily's hot fudge sundae, Penelope wrinkled her nose. "With your spoon?"

"I'll get you a new one!" Rani skipped across the room, snagged a fresh spoon from Rich, and was back at Penelope's side in a moment.

"Here you go!" She plopped the spoon into the ice cream.

Penelope hesitated.

Rani spun away, swooping through the room in circles. Melting blobs of ice cream flew into the air.

Emily nudged her hot fudge sundae a little closer to Penelope.

"Ice cream tastes better up here!" Rani called out. She was standing on top of Mr. Cleary's desk. Somehow, she had acquired a second cone, which she held in her other hand. It had two scoops of chocolate fudge ripple.

When Emily looked back at Penelope, the spoon was in her mouth. Her eyes were closed. She was smiling.

"Here," Emily said softly, pushing the sundae all the way in front of Penelope. "You can have the whole thing."

She left Penelope and ran to the window, where Rich was just about to close the serving hatch.

"One more?" he asked, seeing Emily's face. "You got it!"

Emily sat down at the table with Penelope to eat.

"So long!" Rich called and saluted them all with his ice-cream scoop. Otto leaped out of the truck just before Rich slid the hatch shut.

"I've got a rainbow nose!" Rani shrieked from Mr. Cleary's desk. A blob of orange and purple sherbet slid down her nose and landed in her mouth.

Anson sang "You Ain't Nothing but a Hound Dog" with his Mississippi mud bar for a microphone. Maureen Kenilworth had her cherry slushie in one hand and Dylan Okoshi's ice-cream cone in the other, because Dylan was trying to see if she could do cartwheels from one wall of the room to the opposite one. Whenever Dylan flipped upright, Maureen fed her a bite of rocky road.

Penelope put her sundae cup to her lips and let the dregs of melted vanilla slide down her throat.

Rani waved wildly at Emily and crunched through the cone holding the last of her rainbow sherbet. She flung the second cone, which still had a scoop of chocolate fudge ripple, directly at Emily.

"Catch!" she shrieked.

Emily dropped her sundae on the table, jumped up, and reached out with both hands.

She found herself holding a handful of chilly, gooey creaminess.

"Throw it back!" Rani called.

Emily didn't stop to think. She drew her arm back to throw just as the classroom door opened.

"Grown-up alert!" Anson hollered.

Penelope dropped her empty sundae cup to the floor. Anson flung the stick from his Mississippi mud pop out the window. Kids gulped down the last of their ice cream or gobbled final bites of cone as they whisked into seats at the table.

But Emily turned toward the doorway. She saw Mr. Cleary standing there, his mouth open wide enough to swallow an entire scoop of ice cream in one gulp.

Emily felt frozen in place. Except for her arm. It never stopped moving.

The melting scoop of ice cream sailed into the air. It flew toward the open door.

Mr. Cleary ducked.

Chocolate fudge ripple smacked into the face of Mrs. Pinkney, who was standing behind him.

CHAPTER 26

To Emily, it felt as if years and years had passed since the horrible moment when the ice cream had hit Mrs. Pinkney's face. But she knew it couldn't really have been more than thirty minutes or so.

Inside Mr. Cleary's office, she sat on a yellow beanbag chair. She'd washed her hands, but there wasn't much that could be done about her shirt.

Next to her, Rani was on a beanbag of her own—a blue one. She had her legs stretched out straight in front of her. Humming, she tapped her toes together. Then her heels. Then her toes again.

Mrs. Pinkney was still cleaning herself up. Mr. Cleary had taken her to the teachers-only bathroom.

Emily knew she would never forget how slowly the ice cream had slid down Mrs. Pinkney's face. Soft, melty blobs had clung to her eyebrows. The rest had slithered down her cheeks and drizzled all over the front of her blouse until it finally, finally, plopped to the floor, all while Emily had stared and Jonah Pinkney's mouth had changed from an astonished O to a delighted grin.

"Wow!" he'd shouted.

Now Mrs. Pinkney was trying to get all that ice cream off. When she came back, what would happen then?

That was the question.

Emily had been in Mr. Cleary's office lots of times. There had been that morning, of course, with Rani and her mother. Other times she had delivered notes from teachers and picked up papers or books that had to be taken back to the classroom. On her ninth birthday she had brought Mr. Cleary one of her dad's chocolate-cream-cheese cupcakes.

But she'd never sat on the beanbag chairs before. The beanbags were where you sat if Mr. Cleary wanted to have a special conversation with you.

In other words, if you were in trouble.

Emily had never had a special conversation with the principal. She'd never needed a fresh start.

Her stomach felt very strange, heavy and hollow at the same time. Rani's humming was starting to make it feel worse.

Didn't she understand how serious this was?

Could Rani *ever* be serious? About anything?

"Rani!" she burst out all of a sudden. "Can you—"

Rani looked over at her like a startled puppy.

". . . not hum?" Emily mumbled. She stared down at her hands. Even after soap and water, they were still a little sticky.

"Okay," Rani said. She began to sing. "The itsy bitsy spider went up the water spout. Down came the rain—"

"*Rani!*" Emily said.

Rani stopped singing.

The door opened. Mr. Cleary came in.

Emily's heavy, hollow stomach got heavier and oozed down toward her toes.

Mr. Cleary sat, a little awkwardly, on a red beanbag. He had very long legs, and he had to work a little bit to get them crossed properly.

"Now," he said. "Rani. Emily."

"I'm sorry," Emily said quickly. "I'm so sorry. I didn't mean to hit Mrs. Pinkney with the ice cream. I didn't throw it at her. Not on purpose. Really. I'm sorry."

Rani seemed concerned. "Doesn't Mrs. Pinkney like chocolate fudge ripple?" she asked. She started to get up. "I think Rich is still outside. I could go get her some mint chocolate chip."

Mr. Cleary sighed. "I think we need—"

But he didn't get a chance to finish.

Emily had never thrown ice cream at a grown-up before. She had also never interrupted the principal. But she did now.

"Rani!" she nearly yelled. "You can't go get her mint chocolate chip!"

Rani patted her red backpack. "Sure I can. I have plenty of—"

"It's not because of money!" Emily said, just as loudly as before. "Rani, you can't *do* stuff like this. All the time! You're breaking the rules all the time! I keep trying to help you. But you don't listen to me! You don't listen to anybody! And now we're in trouble! Rani, haven't you ever been in trouble before?"

Slowly, Rani's face changed from cheerful to baffled to anxious. She shook her head.

"Emily," Mr. Cleary said gently.

"I'm in trouble too!" Emily wailed. "And it's your fault! I'm in trouble because of you!"

Rani turned to Mr. Cleary. "Is Emily in trouble?" she asked.

Mr. Cleary sighed again.

"Here at Henrietta Minnow, we try not to talk about being in trouble," he said. "But I think there's something more than ice cream going on right now."

Rani began to look a little hopeful. "Chocolate cake too?"

Emily groaned. There was a knock on the door.

"Yes, come in, please," Mr. Cleary called.

Mrs. Pinkney opened the door, holding Jonah by the hand. Her blouse was still damp and covered with sticky brown splotches.

Behind her, Emily could see her own parents.

CHAPTER 27

Emily and Rani were sent into the hall. Penelope was already there, on the bench next to the office door. She had a smear of fudge on her chin.

Mr. Cleary nudged Jonah out after them.

"Why don't you three take Jonah to the playground?" he asked. "No, no, I'm sure it'll be fine," he said to someone inside the office. "They're very responsible girls—"

"Responsible!" exploded Mrs. Pinkney.

Mr. Cleary quickly shut the door.

Without a word, Penelope got to her feet. She took Jonah's hand and marched down the hallway toward the door that led to the playground.

Because she didn't know what else to do, Emily followed. Rani trailed behind.

Outside, Jonah's eyes widened at the sight of Rich's ice cream truck, still parked by the gates. Otto sat nearby, as if waiting patiently for something, and Mr. Hayes, the custodian, was talking to Rich through the window.

Jonah started toward the truck, but Penelope snagged the sleeve of his bright red T-shirt and steered him toward the sandpit instead.

Jonah cast one mournful look at the truck, plopped down in the sand, and started to dig a series of slow, deliberate holes. He took a green plastic figure from his pocket, a froglike man with webbed feet, and dropped the toy into one of his holes. He buried it. Then he dug it up again.

Emily sat down on one of the tree stumps that had been arranged around the sandpit and stared at Jonah. They were supposed to watch him, after all.

Penelope sat too. Rani stood, fidgeting with the straps of her backpack. "I think I've had about enough education for one day," she announced.

She turned on one heel and began to walk slowly toward the playground gates. Atop the flagpole, her orange scarf still waved merrily in the breeze.

Emily couldn't believe it. How could Rani *still* not understand what to do? She took one small step in the other girl's direction and then hesitated.

"You should let her go," Penelope said.

Emily studied Rani's shoulders, slumped under the weight of her backpack. For the first time the load seemed too heavy for such a small girl.

"She'll just get you in trouble if you go after her," Penelope told her. "*More* trouble."

Rani was already halfway across the blacktop. Rich waved and drove off. Mr. Hayes trudged back toward the school building.

"Rani!" Emily called. She jumped up. "Stop!"

Emily hurried to Rani. She grabbed one of her friend's arms with both hands, tugging her back toward the sandpit. "You can't go," Emily said firmly.

"I can't?" Rani asked. She sounded lost. "Why not?"

"Because—" Emily's explanation got stuck in her throat. She tried again, pointing at the school building. "Because they're *talking* about us."

"But they don't need us to do that," Rani said. "They can talk all they like without us. Grown-ups are *good* at talking." She brightened up a little. "Once when I was in Alice Springs, I met a man who had been talking for seventeen hours straight. They had to set up relays of people to listen to him."

"He'd have to stop talking to eat," Penelope pointed out. She'd left her seat on the tree trunk and moved closer to them.

"Nope, he didn't. He switched to using sign language and got someone to hold a sandwich up to his mouth," Rani answered cheerfully.

But when she looked at Emily, the cheerfulness slid off her face.

"I don't think I can manage it, Emily," she said soberly. "All the rules and the education at the same time. Let's go roller skating instead. Or hang gliding maybe."

Emily shook her head.

Maybe Rani would never understand that kids lived in a world made by grown-ups. And that meant kids had to live by grown-up rules.

Even if you lived in an attic with a loft and a slide and a trampoline and a great big dog, that didn't mean that the rules weren't there. Sooner or later, every kid would have to deal with them.

"We *have* to stay," Emily said as patiently as she could. "We don't have a choice. They'd be really worried if they came out and we weren't here."

Rani shook her head just as patiently.

"Grown-ups are good at worrying too," she said.

The door to the school banged open, and Mrs. Pinkney came striding out. Emily's parents and Mr. Cleary followed.

"I've fulfilled my responsibilities, that's all," Mrs. Pinkney said, each word as crisp as the *clack* of her heels on the blacktop. "Penelope, let's go. Where's Jonah?"

Penelope, Emily, and Rani turned to the sandpit. The empty sandpit.

Where *was* Jonah?

CHAPTER 28

"He never wanders off! Never!" Mrs. Pinkney insisted. She clutched her purse and scanned the playground in all directions. "He must be somewhere! I'm sure he's somewhere!"

"Everyone's somewhere," Rani agreed. Emily shook her head at her.

The doors of the school could only be opened from the inside, so Jonah definitely wasn't in the building. And they'd already searched the playground for him.

"Janice, we'll find him," Emily's dad said steadily. "You three didn't see him go anywhere?" he asked, turning to Rani, Emily, and Penelope. "Was he near the gates?"

Emily remembered Jonah playing in the sandpit, but nothing after that. He was so quiet. So small. So easy to overlook.

Miserably, she shook her head. Penelope did the same. Rani was humming "Itsy Bitsy Spider."

Emily's dad turned back to Mrs. Pinkney. "Is there any place nearby that he likes to go? Anything special that might catch his eye?"

There was a pause. Mrs. Pinkney shook her head. Then Penelope spoke up in a low voice.

"I think he . . . wanted some ice cream." She suddenly seemed aware of the smudge of fudge on her chin and rubbed it away with her thumb.

Everyone's head turned toward the street. The school gates were still open. But Rich's truck was nowhere in sight.

Rani reached out a hand, as if she meant to pat Mrs. Pinkney on the arm. "You don't have to be so worried," she said. "Because—"

Mrs. Pinkney swung around to face her. "Stay out of this!" she snapped. "Haven't you done enough?"

Rani's smile vanished. Her hand dropped.

Emily's parents hurried to the gates to look up and down the street. Mr. Cleary ran inside, gasping something about police. Mrs. Pinkney sat down on a tree stump and burst into tears.

Emily had never felt sorry for Mrs. Pinkney before. And she had never felt sorry for Rani before either. She had no idea what to do.

Her mother and father ran back from the gates. Emily's mom sat down next to Mrs. Pinkney and offered her a tissue from her purse. Her dad pointed at Rani and Emily and Penelope.

"Stay on the playground, all three of you," he said, and he strode inside after Mr. Cleary.

Rani seemed restless. She wandered away, past the climber, putting some distance between herself and the sandpit and Mrs. Pinkney. Then she sat down on the bottom end of a slide.

"There really is nothing to worry about," she said, lifting her gaze to Emily's face.

Emily just shook her head again. Rani never worried about anything. How could Emily possibly explain that there were some things actually worth worrying about?

Suddenly Penelope Pinkney was behind her.

"How can you *say* that?" Penelope demanded. "My brother's only four years old! And he's lost in the city all alone!"

"No, he's not," Rani said calmly. "Otto's with him."

"Otto? A dog? Your dog?" Penelope snapped. "You think some dumb dog can take care of a little kid?"

But Otto wasn't dumb. He wasn't an ordinary dog at all, Emily thought with a rush of relief. If Jonah was with Otto, then Jonah really was all right.

"Being lost with a dog is still being lost!" Penelope went on.

"But Otto's never lost," Rani explained. "Sometimes other people don't know where he is, but that's not the same thing. *Otto* always knows where he is." She got up, settling her backpack more securely on her shoulders and turned toward the gates.

"Rani." Emily tried her best to sound firm. "I already told you, we can't go anywhere. They'll all be really worried if we get lost too."

"And *I* already told *you*. Otto never gets lost. But we can go find him if you want. And your little brother too." Rani started off across the blacktop.

Emily looked at Penelope. Penelope looked back at her. Then she glanced across the playground at her mother.

Mrs. Pinkney was still seated on a tree trunk with Emily's mom beside her. Their backs were to Penelope, Emily, and the playground gates.

Penelope returned her gaze to Emily. Her eyes narrowed. "Can she really find Jonah?" she asked.

Emily didn't know what to answer.

Rani could climb up a flagpole. She could build a trampoline and a chicken feeder and a dog hoist. She could summon an ice-cream van to a school window. But could she find Otto and Jonah? Emily wanted to say yes.

But she just wasn't sure.

Penelope seemed to get impatient, waiting for Emily

to answer. She stuck her chin out. It made her face look lumpy and stubborn. "I'm going with her," she announced.

Rani was already on the other side of the school gates. Penelope hurried after her.

Emily couldn't believe it. Or rather, she could easily believe that Rani was leaving the playground after being told not to—but Penelope?

Penelope Pinkney was going with Rani?

Emily knew perfectly well what she should do. She should go tell her mother—no, her mother was busy hunting in her purse for another tissue for Mrs. Pinkney. Well, her father, then. She should find her father and tell him that Rani and Penelope were going to hunt for Jonah. And for Otto too.

Then the grown-ups would stop the two girls. Bring them back. Keep them safe. Nobody else would get lost.

And nobody would find Jonah and Otto.

Because, Emily thought, the grown-ups would never believe that Otto actually was with Jonah—looking after him, keeping him safe. Just like he did with Rani.

And they'd never understand that Rani could really find Otto.

Letting Rani do just that was the quickest way to get Jonah back. To make Mrs. Pinkney feel better. To return everything to normal.

"Wait!" Emily gasped. "I'm coming too!"

CHAPTER 29

Emily felt shivery as she hurried after Rani and Penelope. Her whole back prickled, as if her skin were trying to warn her about the many, many rules she was breaking.

She waited for her mom to call her. Or her dad to come out and notice what was happening. Mr. Cleary or Mr. Hayes would shout her name. Or the gates would clang shut on their own and trap her inside.

But none of that happened. And Emily, along with Rani and Penelope, found herself standing on the sidewalk.

"Which way?" Penelope asked.

Rani pointed toward the corner of the block.

Emily's eyes followed her finger but all she saw was a woman in a purple vest walking a dog with curly white fur.

The dog had its nose to the pavement and was eagerly licking at something.

"So unsanitary," Penelope muttered.

Rani set off at a confident jog. Emily and Penelope followed. The woman tugged her dog away as the three of them reached the corner.

Emily gazed up and down the street. Cars trundled past. Bikes swooped by. People walked or jogged with earbuds in their ears. A dad pushed a stroller. A teenager teetered along on a unicycle.

There was no sign of a four-year-old or a big black dog.

Penelope folded her arms and glared at Rani. "Why do you even think Jonah went this way?"

But Rani was busy inspecting a sticky patch of sidewalk.

Emily suddenly realized what the white dog had been licking—a gooey orange blob melting across the concrete.

"Jonah wanted ice cream!" Emily exclaimed.

Penelope was now studying the blob too. "That's the kind he likes," she said slowly. "The orange kind. With rainbow sprinkles. Look!"

A scattering of sprinkles had drifted along the sidewalk, as if Jonah had turned the corner and continued down the block.

"The bookstore," Penelope said. She was pointing at a storefront about halfway down the street. "He likes the bookstore."

She set off at a run.

In the store's front window, a model train wove its way in and out among books. "He always stops to watch this train," Penelope said, puffing a little as they came up to the window.

She shoved the bookstore's door open and disappeared inside. Emily saw her talking to the person at the counter. In another minute, Penelope was back.

"He's not in there," she said. "But that lady said she saw a kid in a red T-shirt looking in the window a little while ago."

The model train chugged underneath a tall picture book that had been propped open to make a tunnel. Penelope started searching up and down the sidewalk again. Rani gazed at the sky, rose up on her toes, bent one knee, and spun in a pirouette.

"Rani?" Emily asked. "Which way should we go?"

Rani lowered her bent leg to the ground behind her and swept a curtsey, spreading her pink skirt wide. "Don't know," she said.

"You don't know?"

Emily's stomach wobbled. She glanced back to the corner where the ice cream blob still sat on the sidewalk.

Should they retrace their steps to the Henrietta Minnow School? They'd found out something about Jonah, after all. They could tell Mrs. Pinkney and Emily's parents and Mr. Cleary and everybody. . . .

The door of the bookstore swung open as a customer hurried out. Reflected in its glass, Emily caught a glimpse of something red. She whirled around.

But it wasn't Jonah. It was just a bright red scooter propped against the front stoop of a three-story apartment building a little farther down the block.

A scooter . . .

"Jonah really liked that scooter in the SuperSmart-SaverMart," Emily said. "Remember, Rani?"

Rani bounced up from her curtsey, smiling. In less than a minute they were all grouped around the scooter.

But there wasn't a store clerk here to talk to. Nobody to ask if they'd seen a little boy and a big black dog.

Above them, at the top of the steps, a door banged open.

"Hey!" called a familiar voice. "What are you guys doing?"

CHAPTER 30

Emily's heart jolted in her chest and then jittered down to a steadier rhythm as she saw Anson at the top of the steps.

Rani kept on doing pirouettes. Penelope was looking up and down the block, and she never talked to Anson, anyway. So it seemed to be up to Emily to explain.

"Penelope's little brother got lost," she said. "We're trying to find him. He's somewhere with Rani's dog."

"That big black dog?" Anson asked. "There was a dog like that in the park. Drinking out of the fountain."

He pointed across the street. A triangle of ground on the corner of the block had been planted with grass and decorated with a few tubs of geraniums. In the middle a small fountain bubbled and sloshed.

Penelope spun around. "Was there a boy with the dog? In a red T-shirt?"

Anson shrugged. A silver car swished past, then a blue one.

"Jonah knows he has to hold somebody's hand to cross the street," Penelope said.

"But Otto doesn't have any hands," Rani pointed out. "He has paws."

Penelope snorted, waited for a tandem bike to pass, and hurried across the street to the park. Emily and Rani followed, and to her surprise, Emily realized that Anson was behind her. "What are you doing?" she asked as they reached the fountain.

"I don't want to miss this!" Anson said. "Seriously, is your dog, like, a rescue dog?" he asked Rani. "Can he track people and stuff?"

Rani beamed. "Of course he can!" she said. "Once he—"

Emily interrupted before Rani could tell about what Otto had once done. "But you didn't ask your parents!" she told Anson.

"So? Did you ask yours?"

Emily didn't want to answer. A weak, watery sense of helplessness started to rise inside her, beginning in her knees and creeping upward.

She hadn't kept an eye on Jonah when she'd been told to. She'd left the playground without permission. And after all that, they couldn't even be sure if the dog Anson had seen was really Otto.

And if the dog really had been Otto, was Jonah still with him? If the two were actually still together, how would four fourth graders figure out where they'd gone next?

Penelope seemed to be having some doubts of her own. She folded her arms and glared at Rani. "You said your dog's with my brother. You said you could find your dog. But maybe you can't. And maybe he's not. Maybe you made the whole thing up. Like you make everything up."

Rani gazed back at her. "I make everything up?"

Penelope rolled her eyes. "You know you do. Everybody knows you do." She turned to Emily. "Even you know she makes stuff up. Don't you?"

Emily opened her mouth.

Of course she knew it. Hippos did not eat peanut butter sandwiches. Orangutans did not drink tea—or coffee either. Nobody dreamed on drifting icebergs in the Arctic night.

Emily knew that. But . . .

She also knew that girls did not live alone in attics, or rappel down brick walls, or build trampolines from deflated snowmen, or ride scooters through the SuperSmartSaverMart.

Inside Emily's brain, it felt as if she were swooping between fact and fiction. Truth and lies. Penelope and Rani.

Before Emily could land on one side or the other, Anson stepped forward.

"Hey! I used to have one of these!" He picked up something small and green and damp sitting on the rim of the fountain.

Penelope grabbed it from his hand. "That's Frogman! Jonah loves Frogman!"

"Look," Emily said a little faintly.

Water had slopped over the edge of the fountain, making a puddle. Leading out of the puddle were two sets of damp footprints . . . one made by small sneakers and one made by big paws.

The prints crossed in front of the fountain, vanished in the grass, reappeared on the sidewalk, wandered along a curb, and disappeared on the black asphalt of the road. Jonah had crossed another street.

Emily was surprised to see Mr. Rose's deli on the other side of the road. She hadn't even realized that they were so close to home. Was that where Jonah and Otto had gone next?

Rani seemed to think so. "Mr. Rose keeps treats to give to all the dogs," she said, and hopped off the curb.

There was no big black dog sniffing the bunches of bananas or the piles of apples set out on tables along the sidewalk. No little boy peering around buckets of tulips and roses.

But Mr. Rose was there, filling up a bin with carnations. "Hi, Rani!" he said cheerfully.

Rani waved, snatched up an orange, and began peeling it. "Did Otto come by for his biscuit today?" she asked.

"She just took an orange! Can she do that?" Anson asked Emily.

Emily shrugged.

"Sure he did," Mr. Rose answered Rani. "Had a little kid with him. Friend of yours?"

"My brother!" Penelope burst out. "And he's lost. Where'd they go?"

"Didn't seem lost," Mr. Rose said. "They went right down that alley like they knew just where they were going." He pointed the way with a dripping bunch of flowers.

"Thanks!" Rani snatched up a second orange, tossed it to Anson, and skipped toward the alley.

Emily had never been down this alley before. Empty plastic crates were piled along a side wall of the deli, and scraps of cabbage leaves and bits of old labels and sodden paper bags squelched underfoot.

Rani and Anson added their orange peels to the litter.

Penelope frowned. "I don't think Jonah would come back here," she muttered as they made their way ahead.

"Oh, I think he would," Rani answered cheerfully.

Penelope bristled. "How would you know?" she demanded. "He's my brother. Not yours." The alley turned a corner. Now the back of a shoe repair store ran along one side. On the other was a wooden fence.

"And my mom would never let him go anywhere like this," Penelope went on. "There's dirt. There's trash. There's—"

Rani stopped alongside a fencepost. Beside it, two wooden slats had been broken off. A tuft of shaggy black fur was snagged on the splintery edge of one board.

"There's chickens!" Rani finished triumphantly.

Emily stared through the hole in the fence at her own backyard.

There was the brick patio. There was the coop for Araminta, Betty, and Carlotta. There was the whirligig Rani had made for them, twirling in a stately circle under a gentle breeze.

Beside it sat Otto, his tail wagging gently. Jonah Pinkney crouched beside him, a wide smile on his face, blobs of orange ice cream on his shirt, scattering bits of crumbled-up dog biscuit in the dirt for the chickens to eat.

CHAPTER 31

Now, everything would be all right.

All they had to do, Emily thought, was get Jonah back to the school playground. Mrs. Pinkney would stop crying. Mr. Cleary would stop worrying. (Well, Emily had to admit that Mr. Cleary would probably never stop worrying.) Emily's own parents would calm down. And things would go back to normal.

As normal as they could get with Rani around.

But nobody else seemed to understand how important it was to hurry back to the Henrietta Minnow school.

Penelope was busy hugging and scolding her brother. Anson was examining the whirligig. Otto was panting gently with the tip of his tail swishing back and forth. Rani was . . . What was Rani doing?

Buckling on her climbing harness, which hung down from the roof of the building on a long line.

"Um," Emily said. "Rani? It's sort of a bad time to do that."

Rani fastened a buckle. "Oh, I don't think that three forty-two in the afternoon is such a bad time," she said. "Not like eleven fifty-nine. You really have to keep an eye on that one."

"And you're never, ever, ever supposed to cross the street by yourself!" Penelope said to Jonah, who emptied his last fistful of crumbs over one of the whirligig's funnels.

"But, Rani, we have to—"

"Or seven seventeen!" Rani continued. She bent down to pick up Araminta and tucked the feathery bundle inside her red backpack.

"Hey, did you build this thing?" Anson asked.

"See you later!" Rani said, waving to everyone. "More fun and friendship!"

She turned and began to hoist herself up the wall. From inside the backpack, Araminta gave several approving clucks.

"Whoa." Anson stared as Rani headed upward. "Where's she going?"

Emily ignored him and leaned down a little to take hold of Jonah Pinkney's sticky hand.

"Time to go," she said.

Penelope took Jonah's other hand. Together they towed the little boy along as he craned his neck to watch Rani, who had reached the second floor. Otto got up, shook himself all over, and trotted behind them.

Anson followed Otto, walking backward so he, too, could keep an eye on Rani. He didn't take his gaze off her even when he tripped over Betty and landed on top of her. She escaped with an explosion of furious clucking.

"Anson, shake a tail feather!" Emily called over her shoulder. "We have to get back to school!"

But it turned out that they didn't.

Mrs. Pinkney, Mr. Cleary, and Emily's parents had not stayed on the school playground. As Emily and Penelope led Jonah around to the front of the apartment building, they found all four grown-ups hurrying down the sidewalk toward them. A police officer was walking behind them and a black-and-white car had just pulled up to the curb.

A second officer got out of the car. "You said there was a lost kid?" he asked the first one. Both took in the hugging, admonishing, and explaining that was going on all around them.

"A bunch of them," she answered. "Looks like they all got found."

The officer who'd come on foot took a small notebook from her pocket. "Can I just get some—" But she didn't finish her thought. She was staring at the top of the apartment building and had gone very still.

"Everyone stay calm," she said in a quiet, urgent voice. "We can't startle her. No noise, all right? Let me handle this."

The faces of everyone in the group turned up to find Rani standing on the roof of the apartment building.

She waved.

Mr. Cleary cupped both hands to his mouth. "Don't move! Come down! We'll come get you!" he shouted.

"I said no noise!" the police officer snapped.

"It's okay," Emily said. "Really. She does this kind of thing all the time."

Nobody appeared to find this reassuring.

"Get down from there this instant!" Mrs. Pinkney shrieked.

"Will you all just—" the police officer started, but she was interrupted by a long, clear yodel.

It came from Rani. She spread her arms wide and sprang off the roof.

In an elegant swan dive, Rani plummeted toward the ground. Everyone stood frozen with horror. Even Emily held her breath.

When Rani's head was just a few yards from the ground, the bungee cord around her ankles snapped her back up into the air. She plunged earthward again, bounded back up into the sky, and at last came to rest, bobbing gently upside down with her face on a level with Mr. Cleary's.

"Wow," Jonah and Anson whispered together.

"Oh, hello," Rani said to Mr. Cleary. "Did you need me to come back to the school and help out with the club again? I'm exhilarated now, by the way. How are you feeling?"

"Lord have mercy," one of the police officers murmured. He sank down on the bench beside the front door and put a hand over his heart.

"Rani, come down from there," Emily's father told her in his teacher voice.

He helped unfasten the rubber cord from around Rani's ankles and turned her right side up. Then he lowered her to the ground. Otto came to her side and nosed at her cheek.

Rani stood blinking up at the adults surrounding her. Slowly her smile faded.

"Is something wrong?" she asked.

CHAPTER 32

Mr. Cleary put a hand to his forehead. He took in a very deep breath. He let it out extremely slowly.

Then he knelt down on the sidewalk so he was face-to-face with Rani.

"Rani," he said. His voice came out a little wobbly, but it firmed up with his next sentence. "Nothing is wrong. We're all here to help you."

Rani gave the principal her widest smile. "How nice of you," she said. "But I don't need any help right now. Thanks all the same."

"Sometimes we don't realize when we need help," Mr. Cleary went on. "But a lot of people are very worried."

"I'm sorry you're worried. Would you like to try bungee jumping?" Rani offered. "It always cheers me up."

Mr. Cleary glanced up at the apartment building and shuddered. "Now, Rani, a child of your age needs parents. And I hear—"

"Oh, I have parents." Rani sounded relieved. "You don't have to worry about *that.* One, at least. You can get by with one, right? Two is nice if you need a spare, but one will do."

Mr. Cleary began to get the slightly wide-eyed expression that was becoming familiar to Emily. It was the way grown-ups tended to look when they talked to Rani.

The police officer who was still standing up moved a little closer, as if she wanted to overhear what was being said.

"But I understand that your mother's not always at home," Mr. Cleary went on. "And little girls can't live alone."

"Of course not. I'm never alone. Otto's always around."

"Otto?" Mr. Cleary shook his head a little in bewilderment. "Who's Otto? Does he take care of you?"

"Sure he does. And I take care of him too. I put his food

in his bowl . . ." Rani's voice trailed off as she caught sight of Emily vigorously shaking her head.

"You put his food in a bowl?" Mr. Cleary blinked. "Can I meet this Otto, please?"

"Of course!" Rani draped an arm around Otto's shoulders. "He loves to meet new people."

Otto offered his paw to Mr. Cleary, who took it automatically.

"Yes, very nice," he said, dropping the paw. "But where is Otto, Rani?"

Rani gave him a pitying look. "Right here," she said gently, as if she thought Mr. Cleary was pleasant but not very bright.

Jonah Pinkney edged closer to Otto, who gave him a paw also. Emily could tell what was going to happen next.

Rani was about to explain everything to Mr. Cleary—that Otto was a dog, that her mom was in Patagonia, that Rani lived in an attic and slept in a hammock where the dreams were almost as good as the ones you got on a drifting iceberg.

And what would happen after that? Emily was sure it would be nothing good.

"Rani!" she blurted as Rani beamed at Mr. Cleary and opened her mouth.

Everyone turned to stare at Emily.

What should she say? How could she possibly help Rani now?

Then, suddenly, she knew.

"Rani, where's Mr. Armand?" she asked.

Rani shrugged.

"We've been trying to call him all afternoon!" Emily's mother said. "He's not answering his phone. I don't know what's wrong."

Mr. Cleary seemed to relax a bit. "So Otto's last name is Armand?" he asked.

Emily's father spoke up. "Well, not exactly—" he began.

"Oh, for goodness's sake!" Mrs. Pinkney snapped. "Claude Armand's first name is *not* Otto. Otto is that *dog*. And it's high time that someone took control of this situation." She stepped forward, seized Jonah's arm, and pulled him away from Otto.

Her other hand reached for Rani's shoulder. Emily couldn't tell what she planned to do. Push Rani away from Otto? Just keep Rani still while she dragged Jonah away?

Emily never figured it out, because before Mrs. Pinkney's hand touched Rani, Otto was between them, a sleek black mountainous mass of dog.

Mrs. Pinkney snatched Jonah back with a yelp of alarm.

"It growled at me!" she gasped. "That dog *growled* at me!"

"No, he didn't," Emily said. She was quite close to Otto and she hadn't heard a single growl.

"Yeah, he really didn't." Anson tried his best to back Emily up.

Nobody seemed to hear what they'd said.

"The dog? Otto is the *dog*?" Finally Mr. Cleary understood.

"Penelope, Jonah, come inside this instant!" Mrs. Pinkney ordered.

"Janice, I don't think the dog is actually dangerous," Emily's mom said soothingly.

"Don't you tell me that. I'm the one it growled at!"

"Otto never growls!" Emily said a little bit louder.

"Otto is the *dog*?" Mr. Cleary exclaimed again.

Mrs. Pinkney marched Penelope and Jonah into the building. Mr. Cleary smoothed his hair back with both hands, looking as if he'd rather tear it out. The police officer on the bench stood up.

"That dog doesn't have a license. Doesn't even have a collar," he said.

And that, Emily thought later, was when everything really went wrong.

CHAPTER 33

A short time later, Emily and Rani sat in Emily's room. Emily could hear her parents in the kitchen, getting dinner ready. They had turned on some classical music with cellos and bassoons, so only a word or two of what they were saying got through.

". . . for the best, I . . ."

". . . really think so?"

". . . couldn't go on . . ."

All the grown-ups had talked and talked and talked down there in front of the apartment building. After what seemed like a horribly long time to Emily, they'd agreed that Rani could stay with Emily's family for right now, at least until Mr. Armand turned up or someone could track down Rani's mom.

Mr. Cleary had asked a lot of questions about Rani's mom. Where was she in Patagonia, exactly? What was she doing there? When would she be back? Did Rani know her phone number? Her email? Any way to get in touch with her?

But Rani hadn't answered any of those questions.

Rani hadn't said a single word since one of the two police officers had explained that all dogs had to be licensed. She had gently pried Rani's arms away from Otto's neck, led the big dog to the black-and-white car, put him in the back of it, and nodded at the second officer to drive away.

Emily had seen Otto's face as he stared through the car's back window. She did not know who looked more heartbroken—Otto or Rani.

Now Rani sat huddled on Emily's bed. She looked tinier than ever.

And she wasn't talking. Not even to Emily.

Rani. Wasn't. Talking.

"Listen," Emily said to her. "Listen, Rani. The police officer said she had to take Otto to the shelter until we can get a license for him. But we can get him back, okay? When

Mr. Armand gets here. Or your mom. They'll get him a license. It's just for a little while, okay?"

Rani stirred. She turned to face Emily. Her blue eyes seemed faded and dim.

"Why didn't you tell me?" she whispered.

"Tell you what?" What was there to tell? Rani knew everything that had happened. None of it was a secret. What had she expected Emily to tell her?

"About the collar. For Otto. And a license," Rani answered softly. "Why didn't you tell me there was a rule about those things for dogs?"

Emily couldn't think of anything to say.

"If I'd known there was a rule . . ." Rani bent her knees up to her chest and hugged them. She hid her face.

"Rani?" Emily said.

There was no answer.

It had never occurred to Emily that Otto might need a collar. Or a license. Those were for the kind of dog that got taken on walks and sometimes got fleas or jumped up on the counter and ate the lasagna. Otto wasn't that kind of dog.

But the police officers hadn't known that.

"Rani? I'm sorry."

The police officers had only been there because Jonah had left the school playground. And Jonah wouldn't have been on the school playground at all if Emily hadn't thrown the ice-cream cone at Mrs. Pinkney.

"Rani," Emily said. "Rani?"

Rani's mom was so far away. And now she didn't have her dog.

All she had was Emily, who felt like a not-very-good friend. A friend who was so busy trying to get Rani to follow the rules that she'd missed the one that really mattered.

"Just wait here," Emily told Rani. "I'll be back as soon as I can."

Under the cover of a loud moment for the kettledrums in the music from the kitchen, Emily slipped out of the apartment, shutting the door behind her.

She made it down one flight of stairs before she found Penelope sitting gloomily on the landing.

Emily could hear Mrs. Pinkney's voice from inside the apartment.

"She's calling my dad," Penelope said. "She always gets even madder when she calls my dad."

Emily nodded, but she couldn't stop to talk. She sidled past Penelope and kept going. It was only when she opened the front door of the building that she realized Penelope was behind her.

To Emily's surprise, Anson was slouched on the bench outside the front door.

"What are you still doing here?" Penelope asked him.

Anson sat up straighter. "It's boring at my house," he said. "Is Rani coming out?"

Emily shook her head. She wasn't sure how to say, *Rani isn't Rani anymore.*

Then she figured it out. "Rani needs Otto back," she said.

Anson nodded. Penelope made a face.

"Dogs, yuck," she said. "But she did find Jonah like she said she could. So I guess we better go get that dumb dog."

CHAPTER 34

Anson knew where the animal shelter was. "We had to go there when my sister's cat got lost," he explained.

"Can we just say we want to adopt Otto?" Emily asked as they walked. But she knew it would not be that simple.

"They're not going to let some kids just adopt a dog," Penelope told her.

Anson agreed. "You have to have a grown-up. You have to sign things."

"So what are we going to do?" Emily asked.

"Break him out!" Anson grabbed a lamppost and swung in a circle around it. "Like a raid. A rescue. A jailbreak!"

Penelope snorted. "We say he's our dog and then they have to give him back."

Emily was doubtful. "But are they going to believe us? We're just kids, like you said."

"Kids have dogs," Penelope said calmly.

"But . . ."

"Emily." Penelope turned her head to give Emily a look that said, *Stop arguing*. "We have to *try*."

Emily still didn't think they could walk into the shelter and announce that Otto belonged to the three of them . . . but she couldn't come up with anything better. And like Penelope said, they had to try.

They passed an empty playground and a dry cleaner's and a drugstore and a shop that sold flowers and fruit and windchimes. It was the second time this day, Emily thought, that she was walking through her neighborhood without permission.

Anson led them around a corner, and now they were on a block Emily didn't recognize.

They hurried past apartment buildings and a thrift shop and an empty storefront with a blank black doorway that made Emily shiver.

Anson stopped walking and pointed. “There,” he said.

Emily studied the plain, one-story building on the other side of the street. It said City Animal Shelter over the front door.

If Rani were here, Emily thought, she would tap dance into the building. She’d do a backflip or several cartwheels. She’d dazzle the shelter workers with a burst of facts about leopard seals or hippos, and she’d smuggle Otto out through a secret tunnel or parachute him through a window.

But Rani wasn’t here. It was just Emily and Penelope and Anson, and they didn’t have a parachute. Or much of a plan either.

In the distance, Emily heard the jaunty jingle of an ice-cream truck, and it brought back the shuddery horror of the chocolate fudge ripple hitting Mrs. Pinkney in the face. It also made her stomach growl a little. It must be really close to dinnertime.

Emily didn’t know what kind of trouble she might get into if she didn’t show up for dinner, but she was pretty sure it would be even worse than a special conversation. She'd need more than a fresh start.

Maybe they just ought to go home.

"Come *on*," Penelope said, and started across the street. She shoved open the door of the animal shelter and disappeared inside.

Emily traded a nervous glance with Anson. Well, hers was nervous. His was alight with excitement.

As soon as they opened the shelter's door, Emily could hear barking. It bellowed and boomed around her, though there was not a single dog in sight.

They were in a mostly bare room with a counter along one side. Penelope was standing in front of the counter, giving the woman behind it a firm look.

"I'm here to get my dog," she announced. "He's big. Really big. And black. And kind of slobbery, and he doesn't smell that nice."

The woman seemed confused. She had a name tag on. It read, I'M MARGERY! ASK ME ABOUT ADOPTION!

Margery glanced at the door behind Penelope. "Your parents are here too?"

Penelope sounded irritated. “He’s *my* dog,” she said. “Not my parents’ dog. That’s why I came. His name’s Oscar. I mean Otto. Big. Big and black.”

While Penelope talked, Emily let her gaze wander around the room. There was a grubby yellow couch in one corner and a bench with a few magazines on it. That was it, unless you counted a window with a view of the street and a door in the wall behind Margery.

“No, he doesn’t *have* a collar, that’s the whole *problem*!” Penelope was saying. “I’ll get him one. But I can’t get a collar if I don’t have a dog, so—”

“Listen,” Margery interrupted. Emily wasn’t sure which of the two sounded more annoyed. “Just go home and get one of your parents, okay?”

She stepped out from behind the counter. Anson quickly moved to one side. He snagged Emily’s sleeve and tugged her with him.

“That’s not very nice, keeping someone’s dog away from them,” Penelope grumbled. “I don’t think that’s what a shelter should do.”

Margery reached for Penelope's shoulder and steered her toward the front door. "Hey, you're not supposed to touch me!" Penelope snapped.

Anson dragged Emily behind the counter and drew her down to the floor. The door that led to the back of the shelter was right behind them.

"Strangers aren't supposed to touch kids! Don't you know *anything*?" Penelope went on. "I don't think you—"

Anson eased the door open. He oozed through it, and Emily just couldn't stay there crouched behind the counter.

So she followed him.

CHAPTER 35

The noise of frantic dogs exploded into Emily's ears. It was fantastic, the noise. It was unbelievable.

They were standing at one end of a long corridor lined on either side with kennels. Each kennel had a food and water dish, a scrap of blanket, and a dog who clearly believed that the arrival of Emily and Anson was the most exciting thing that had ever happened.

Dogs who had been snoozing woke. Dogs who had been lying on their blankets sat up. Dogs who had been pacing raced to the gates of their kennels.

Dogs who had been quiet started barking.

The noise thundered at Emily. It bounced off the cement floor and the cinderblock walls and thundered at her again. It got inside her head, banging every thought out of her brain.

On her right was a kennel with a litter of puppies, all white frizz and black eyes. A little way down, a hound with a sad, sagging face lifted up his chin and let out more of a yodel than a bark. A beagle flung both front paws at the gate of its kennel, yelping something that clearly meant, "At last! At last! You're here at last!"

Next to the beagle was Otto.

He sat calmly by the gate of his kennel and gazed at Emily and Anson as if he'd been expecting them.

Anson flashed a grin at Emily and ran toward him. Emily stayed where she was, frozen by the deafening noise and the knowledge that she was in a place she was not supposed to be.

Even through the din, her ears caught the sound of the door opening behind her.

"What is all this racket?" asked Margery as she peeked inside. Then she turned her head. "No, look, kid, I already told you, you can't get your dog now," she said over her shoulder.

Emily's feet still felt frozen, but her hand moved. Fascinated, she watched it reach out to the gate of the nearest kennel. Her fingers lifted the latch.

A blizzard of white puppies blew out and swirled around Emily's feet. Emily ducked behind the door to the lobby as it swung all the way open. The puppies darted through.

"Blitzen! Dasher! Dancer!" Margery shouted. "What are you doing? Get back here!"

Emily eased the door shut behind the last of the puppies as they dashed out. Then she ran to Anson's side.

Anson had Otto's kennel open. Otto licked Emily's hand and sniffed Anson's face.

"Back door!" Anson shouted. He pointed. There was another door at the far end of the corridor.

Emily nodded. They hurried past whining dogs and barking dogs and dogs who just watched with sad, abandoned eyes.

Emily grabbed the knob and twisted. It didn't move.

She tugged frantically at the door. Two retrievers, one yellow and one black, boomed at her from opposite kennels. "Outside? Outside?" they seemed to be saying. "Take me! Take me!"

Tugging on a locked door wasn't going to do any good. Emily shook her head at Anson. They'd have to get out through the front.

She turned and realized that Otto was not beside them. He stood in front of the beagle's kennel. As Emily watched, he took the latch of the gate gently in his teeth and tugged it open.

The beagle bounded out, ears flapping.

Other dogs were already milling in the aisle—the hound with the saggy face, a black Lab wiggling from nose to tail, a long skinny dog skidding under Otto's belly to touch noses with a curly-tailed mutt, and something like an animated mop skittering around under everybody's paws.

The door to the lobby swung wide. Margery stood there with two wiggling puppies in her arms and three more yapping about her ankles.

"What is going on?" she bellowed.

If Rani had been there, Emily thought, she would have known what to do.

Rani would have explained to Margery that everything was fine. Rani would have found a long pole and used it to vault over Margery's head. Rani would have done something completely ridiculous that would have turned out to be the perfect thing to do.

Margery piled her armload of yapping white puppies into the nearest kennel and shut the gate. "You two!" she said threateningly. "Get all of these dogs back into their cages this minute!"

But Rani wasn't here, and the back door was still locked, and Penelope was nowhere to be seen, and a collie had just put its front paws onto Anson's shoulders. Anson toppled and the collie began a thorough job of licking his face with a long pink tongue.

So if anyone was going to do anything here, it seemed to be up to Emily. And there was only one thing she could think of.

"No," she said to Margery.

CHAPTER 36

Emily's "no" came out as more of a squeak than a word, and Emily was pretty sure Margery couldn't hear it over the barking, baying, yipping, whining, and howling. But Margery probably heard the next thing that came out of Emily's mouth, because Emily shrieked it at the top of her lungs.

"Otto! Run!"

Otto obeyed as if she were Rani.

Suddenly a black blur was racing down the aisle. He sailed gracefully over two wrestling retrievers, dodged the skittering mop-ish dog, and headed straight for Margery.

She ducked.

Otto leaped over her.

Emily seized Anson's arm and yanked him up.

While Margery was gaping after Otto, Emily and Anson tore down the aisle toward her. Emily nearly tripped over the mop-ish dog, so she scooped it up in her arms. Two black eyes glittered up at her through gray fluff. A tiny pink tongue panted.

The collie lollopped behind Anson, clearly thinking this was a delightful game. Anson scrambled around the retrievers and tripped over the long-eared hound while Emily came face-to-face with Margery.

"Here," Emily said as politely as she could.

She handed the mop-ish dog to Margery, who took it automatically. Emily ducked past on her left, while Anson stumbled by on the right.

Both of them burst out into the lobby and around the counter. "Get back here!" Margery cried.

Nobody did as she said. The two kids slammed open the door and ran out to the sidewalk. Gasping, Emily looked around for Otto. And where was Penelope?

She didn't see either one. But she did see a white cylinder, about a foot long, rolling along the sidewalk toward them.

Behind Emily, dogs exploded out of the shelter, a barking, joyful mass of fur and paws. Several pounced on the white cylinder. Some stuck their muzzles inside. Others lapped at a sticky white goo oozing out onto the sidewalk.

Ice cream, Emily realized. The thing rolling along the pavement was a tub of ice cream.

And now more tubs were rolling toward them, and more dogs were pouncing on the treats. Emily finally spotted Penelope waving frantically from the back of a white truck.

An ice-cream truck. Rich's ice-cream truck.

Otto was standing beside the truck. He gazed calmly at Emily and Anson as Penelope heaved a tub of sea-salted caramel down the sidewalk. "Go!" Penelope shouted. "Run!"

Margery, open-mouthed, stumbled out of the shelter, still holding the mop-ish dog, which squirmed out of her arms to leap into a puddle of strawberry swirl.

Anson vaulted over the sad-eyed hound, whose long ears were dragging in a pool of vanilla sludge. Emily dodged a greyhound and a poodle, both trying to get their noses inside the same tub of raspberry ripple.

Then they were at the ice-cream truck, and Emily half fell inside next to Penelope.

"Otto, up here!" she panted.

Otto placed his front paws inside the truck. He didn't appear to be in any hurry.

Margery was running now, but her foot slipped in a creamy smear. She staggered to one side.

Anson grabbed Otto's massive hindquarters and heaved. The big dog didn't budge.

"Otto, come on!" Emily begged.

Otto studied her gravely, licked her nose, and jumped nimbly into the truck. Penelope and Emily had to scoot aside to make room.

Anson flung himself in after Otto.

Margery had caught her balance. A grayish terrier danced around her, yapping.

"You kids!" she shouted. "Get that dog back where he belongs!"

So Emily did just what Rani would have done.

"Okay!" she called back. "We will!" Then she slammed the truck's door shut.

Rich, in the driver's seat, revved the engine. "Ready to go, kids?" he called back.

"Ready!" Penelope shouted.

The truck lurched forward. Anson fell on Emily, who toppled into a freezer.

Beneath her, something yipped.

Otto didn't even sway. He licked a few drips of vanilla from his whiskers.

"Emily, be careful!" Penelope said as Emily scooted to one side and discovered that she'd fallen on one of the fluffy white puppies. The little dog didn't seem to hold any kind of grudge. She wagged up at Emily as if asking what game they were going to play next.

Penelope picked up the puppy, settling it carefully on her lap. "What?" she asked when she noticed Emily staring.

"I thought you didn't like dogs?" Emily said. She felt as if she were trembling all over, but when she checked her hands, they were steady.

"People are allowed to change their minds," Penelope informed her.

"All right back there?" Rich shouted from the front.

"Great! Anson yelled back. He had found a squashed fudgsicle and was busy tugging off the mangled paper.

"Am I taking you kids home?" Rich asked.

All three said yes, but all of a sudden Emily felt drenched in a cold and sticky wave of doubt.

She supposed they had to go home. What other choice was there?

But Otto still didn't have a collar. He didn't have a license. What were they supposed to do about that?

CHAPTER 37

Anson was full of schemes to smuggle Otto up to the attic. Penelope thought it would be better to hide Otto in the backyard with the chickens.

Emily couldn't believe either of those plans would work. But Otto seemed to have his own idea in mind.

Once Rich stopped the truck, Otto sat up and stared at the back door. Emily could see he was expecting her to open it.

She did so.

Otto bounded lightly to the pavement. He wagged his tail back and forth, as if to say thanks, and then headed toward the apartment building.

Emily climbed out too, followed by Anson and Penelope. Penelope still held the small white puppy, now asleep in her arms.

Rich rolled down the driver's side window and pointed at a family of three on the other side of the street. "Customers," he said. "Mind if I take off?"

Emily nodded. She thought it was best for Rich to get his truck out of sight before Mrs. Pinkney showed up. Reminding Mrs. Pinkney about the existence of ice cream was probably a bad idea.

"Thanks," she said to Rich. "Really."

Rich nodded. "Tell Rani I said hi." Then he drove off.

"What now?" Anson asked.

Before anyone could answer, something tumbled out of the attic window—a long coil of purple rope that unrolled as it fell. When one end smacked the ground, Emily saw that Otto's dog harness was attached to it.

Otto walked to the harness. He sniffed it. He looked at Emily with a tilt to his head.

Rani was back in her attic. Emily felt a flicker of hope.

"What's that thing?" Penelope asked.

Emily knelt beside Otto and buckled him into the harness. "Are you sure?" she asked him. "That window's really high."

Otto turned his head and licked her ear.

Emily nodded. She checked the clip that connected Otto's harness to the rope, and she stepped back.

Otto rose into the air, legs dangling. He had just cleared the first floor when the building's front door burst open.

"There you are!" Emily's mother shouted. Her father was behind her, and Mrs. Pinkney was there, too, holding Jonah tightly by the hand. To Emily's surprise, Mr. Cleary was with them.

"Uh, I'm going to head home," Anson muttered. He disappeared just as Emily's mother swept her up in a hug.

Emily hugged her back, taking the opportunity to peek over her mom's shoulder and see Otto clambering into an attic window.

"You see, Janice?" Emily's dad said to Mrs. Pinkney. "I told you they'd be all right. They were together."

Emily's mom swapped her to her father for another hug, and Mrs. Pinkney swooped in on Penelope. "Never, never, never dare to do anything like that again!" Mrs. Pinkney declared, squeezing her daughter tightly.

There was a loud yip.

"Careful, mom!" Penelope wiggled free. "Don't squash her!"

Everybody looked at the white puppy in Penelope's arms, who was wagging her tail so hard her entire body wiggled. She seemed delighted to find herself surrounded by so many new friends.

"Penelope Pinkney, what is *that*?" her mother demanded.

"My dog," Penelope said firmly.

"Your . . . what?"

Jonah came close to his sister and tugged gently on her arm. She lowered the dog to his level. The puppy licked his nose.

"Wow," Jonah whispered, soft but clear. "What's her name?"

"Vanilla," Penelope answered. "Her name is Vanilla."

Mrs. Pinkney slowly shut her mouth. She looked at the dog cuddled in Penelope's arms and at the joy beaming off Jonah's face.

"Well," she said uncertainly. "Well, come upstairs, you two. Both of you. We'll discuss . . ." She let her voice trail off. "Come upstairs."

The Pinkneys hurried inside, leaving Emily and her parents on the sidewalk with Mr. Cleary.

"Where did Penelope get a dog?" Emily's dad asked in bewilderment.

"At the shelter," Emily said.

Both parents focused in on her. "*That's* where the three of you went?" her mother demanded.

Too late, Emily realized her mistake. Now her parents would figure everything out. She'd be in more trouble than ever. And that wasn't even the worst thing.

"To get that dog back?" Emily's father asked.

She could only nod.

The worst thing was that Otto would probably be taken away from Rani all over again.

Her dad sighed. "Emily. I'm sure you thought you were

helping, but you should have left this to the grown-ups." He sighed again. "Where's Otto now?" he asked. "And where's Rani? Isn't she with you?"

Emily couldn't help herself. She glanced up at the attic window.

CHAPTER 38

Just then the door of the first-floor apartment swung open. Mr. Armand stood there, blinking a little, as Emily, her parents, and Mr. Cleary all turned toward him.

"Hello?" he said, as if it were the only comment he could think of.

"We've been trying to call you!" Emily's mother burst out.

"Are you in charge of that child?" Mr. Cleary demanded. "Is your name Otto?"

"Otto is the dog," Emily's father reminded him.

"I was picking up a friend at the airport," Mr. Armand said, looking from face to face. "And I dropped my phone. I'm afraid it did not fare well. May I ask—is something wrong?"

"Wrong!" Mr. Cleary burst out. "Wrong!"

The torrent of explanation that came from all three adults involved ice cream, Capture the Flag, and the animal shelter. Next came chickens, bungee jumping, and something about hippos that even Emily did not understand.

Rani was right. Grown-ups certainly were good at talking.

Mr. Armand stood blinking in more bewilderment than ever. "What is Capture the Flag? Which flag is involved?" he asked.

Mr. Cleary straightened his shoulders. "I have to go inside, please," he said firmly. "I can't leave until I'm sure that child is safe."

Mr. Armand moved aside a little. Emily was about to follow Mr. Cleary when her father put a hand on her shoulder.

"Honey, let's go up to our own apartment," he said.

But Emily pulled her shoulder free from her father's grasp.

"I'm going too," she said. "Rani's my friend."

All week, Emily had been trying to help Rani by teaching her the rules. But trying to teach Rani the rules was like trying to teach a fish to walk on stilts. It was never going to work, no matter how hard you tried. Or how hard the fish tried.

And then Emily had tried to help Rani by breaking the rules. But that hadn't gone well either.

As far as Emily could tell, there was only one thing left that she could do. No matter what was going to happen next, she couldn't let Rani face it without a friend at her side.

So when Mr. Armand held the door open for Mr. Cleary, Emily followed him. Mr. Armand followed Emily. And Emily's parents exchanged a glance and followed Mr. Armand.

Mr. Cleary marched all the way up to the attic and knocked on the door, but there was no answer. He tried the knob. It didn't turn.

"Does anyone have a key?" Mr. Cleary asked.

Emily heard the lock click.

"It's open now," she said. And, indeed, the door swung inward.

Otto was sitting just inside. He wagged the very tip of his tail in a polite manner.

Emily checked the trampoline. It was empty. So was the loft with its pillows and curtains. The chandelier overhead cast flakes of white light and patches of rainbows over the floor.

Everything was just as it usually was, except for one thing.

Rani was not swinging in the hammock or hurtling down the slide or bounding up and down on the trampoline. Instead, she was in the green velvet armchair, curled up in the lap of a woman Emily hadn't met before.

Emily had never seen Rani sit so still.

Even though the woman was a stranger, Emily recognized her. She had long legs in patched pants of faded blue. She wore hiking boots so muddy and dusty it was impossible to tell what color they had once been. She had on a tan vest with pockets everywhere over a purple shirt spangled with mirrors.

The pale skin of her face was scattered with freckles and her red-orange hair frizzed around her head just as Rani's black curls did. Her eyes were as blue as Rani's own.

For a moment they all stood and stared—Emily, her mother and father, and Mr. Cleary. Mr. Armand waved and turned to clump back down the stairs.

"Hi, Emily," Rani called out. She grinned without lifting her head from the red-haired woman's shoulder. "My mom's back from Patagonia!"

CHAPTER 39

After that there was even more talking.

But Emily noticed something funny. Rani's mom was doing very little of the talking herself. Words swooshed and lapped around her like waves, and she listened and nodded now and then.

How could such a quiet mother have a daughter who talked as much as Rani? Maybe it worked out for them, Emily thought. Maybe all the listening Rani's mom did gave Rani's words the space they needed.

When the talking began to get tiresome, Rani and Emily escaped to the loft and hoisted Otto up to join them. They found Araminta roosting on a purple silk cushion embroidered with yellow butterflies. She had an egg underneath her. Otto sniffed at her feathery head.

There was now a dumbwaiter to one side of the loft. Rani turned a crank to pull it up. Inside were a plate of lemon cookies and two glasses of chocolate milk, each with a straw. Rani handed a glass and two cookies to Emily.

Emily took them. The glass was cool in her hand.

Underneath the surprise of seeing Rani's mom, the relief of knowing that Otto was safe, and a touch of worry about what all the grown-ups were talking about this time, she felt a tiny pit of unhappiness deep inside.

So much had happened this afternoon. The finding of Jonah. The rescue of Otto. The arrival of Rani's mom. It took Emily a little while to sort through it all and trace this feeling of unhappiness back to its source.

"Rani?" she asked her friend. "Is your mom going to stay in the attic now?"

The unhappiness quivered a little when she asked the question.

It had been just one week since Emily had met Rani. And a lot of that week had been worrying. Some of it had been scary. But most of it, she thought, had been amazing.

What would happen now? Would everything in Rani's

attic be just as much fun? With a grown-up around all the time?

Emily didn't see how that could possibly be.

"Sure. She gah huh mum hummuck," Rani said through a mouthful of cookie.

Emily thought she understood. "Where will your mom hang her hammock up?" she asked.

Rani swallowed. "Right next to mine."

"Has there always been a trampoline up here?" Emily heard her father ask.

Rani rolled over onto her back, tucked a cookie between her toes, and managed to take a bite. "Until fee goh tuh aw ail uh," she said.

Emily couldn't sort this one out. "What?"

Rani offered the remaining half of her cookie, still between her toes, to Araminta.

"Until she goes to Australia," she said again. "To photograph the giant worms there. They're very shy and hard to take pictures of, so it will be a real challenge. I thought if I sang to them, it might coax them out of their holes. Would they like lullabies do you think? Or opera?"

It was worse than Emily had imagined. Much worse.

She wasn't going to have to get used to having a grown-up around in Rani's attic.

She was going to have to get used to losing her new best friend.

"You're going to Australia?" she asked weakly.

"Well, my mom could use my help with the worms," Rani said. She planted both feet and both hands on the floor of the loft and did a backbend. "So I thought maybe I should."

"I hope you have a good time there," Emily said as politely as she could. "With the worms."

Rani inched over until her head was near her glass of chocolate milk. "Will the milk come out of my nose if I drink it upside down?" she asked.

Emily couldn't answer.

Rani wiggled until the straw was in her mouth and took a drink. "Nope! It goes down! I mean up!" she said. She licked a dribble off her upper lip before it could ooze into her nose. "But then I wondered if we could make a roller-skating rink," she went on. "And how about a trapeze?

Right there?" She picked up one leg to point a toe at the ceiling. "Because I kept thinking . . ."

"Of course education is vital," Mr. Cleary was saying below.

Rani flopped down to lie on the pillows. "About how I've never had friends before," she finished. "It was always just my mom and me and Otto. And we went everywhere, and we saw everything, and we *made* friends, lots of them. But I never got to keep one. Because we always had to leave."

"Oh," Emily said.

Rani sat up and beamed at her. "But then I met you. And you took me to school with you. And shopping. And you got Otto back for me!"

"Anson helped," Emily told her. "Penelope too."

Rani's smile grew wider, which Emily would not have thought was possible. "So I thought I should stay here. And even go to school. For a little education. Not too much. But a little might be fun."

Emily dropped her lemon cookie. Otto, on his belly, inched closer. He picked up the cookie, looked at Emily, and ate it in two bites.

"You're going to stay?" Emily asked.

Rani grinned and nodded.

"All by yourself?" Emily felt a rush of worry underneath a thrill of excitement. If Rani stayed in the attic alone, would the trouble start all over again?

"Of course not by myself," Rani said. "Otto's here!"

Emily nodded. But still . . .

"We're getting him a license right away. And a collar. Do you think they have them at the SuperSmartSaverMart?"

Emily was smiling.

"And I can't be alone when I have Mr. Armand! He says you and your mom and dad can come and have dinner with us anytime if your dad brings cookies. Plus there's Rich! And Mrs. Pinkney and Penelope and Jonah and Anson and you! All my friends!" Rani bounced up to stand on her feet. "Do you think if I jump off from here I could hit the trampoline?"

On her hands and knees, Emily scrambled to Rani's side.

"I bet I'll bounce right up to the ceiling," Rani said, her eyes wide and bright and full of delight.

She spread her arms like a diver on the high board. Emily could see that if she jumped, she'd soar right over the heads of her mom, Mr. Cleary, and Emily's parents.

The trampoline was pretty far away from the loft. Could Rani do it?

Emily thought about telling Rani that the trampoline was too far away. That the grown-ups would be upset. That she might get hurt.

But she decided not to say any of that.

Instead, she looked up at her friend—her friend who was staying. Her smile stretched into a grin.

Could Rani jump as far as the trampoline?

Could she stay in the attic all by herself?

Could she make Penelope into her friend? Maybe even Mrs. Pinkney too?

It didn't seem likely, but Emily had learned one thing for sure in this past week.

With Rani, anything was possible.